TANGLED DESTINATIONS
DEPARTURES

B. HARTLEY

Tangled Destinations
Departures

B. HARTLEY

Acknowledgement

This book was written thinking of the reflection of your soul in my eyes, and the blending of our hearts while we travel the Universe, through infinite time.

All my gratitude to Stephen and Becka.

 One

Navigator Starship:
Warrior I-Cosmos 24x-Infinity

Final Destination...

Leonardo King Baylor, the old patriarch of a wealthy clan was sitting in a lavish leather recliner while holding his helmet in his right hand. The two by two squared meter room was cold and felt sterile. He was wearing the exploration suit designed by the *International Space Confederation*. He got up and took a last look at the recliner, as it disappeared, becoming part of the wall. He was sure this was the last time he would ever set foot in the room. He pushed a green button on his wrist, and answered Victoria's hologram call. The three dimension image of the commander appeared in full color.

"Listen to me. This is the last time I encourage you not to be part of this mission. The androids will complete it. You are not familiar with the program," the woman in the hologram said, concerned, and she continued. "You should stay in the ship and help. Can you hear me?"

His eyes sparkled. No, he couldn't hear well, yet he answered.

"The Council had approved me."

"I can call for a second assembly."

"THERE'S NO MORE TIME, VICTORIA!"

"You better come back in one piece."

"I will!" He sent a goodbye kiss to her and changed the hologram to familiar pictures of Earth. His former residence in Bay Castle, his favorite golf course, and the ocean he loved so much. The 86 year old man was strong enough to complete this mission, although the pain in his lower back was heavier than ever before. He bent down a steel box -his last possession from his planet. He opened the box with reverence and care, and let his eyes to tear with emotion. There it was, his lifetime companion. A fine guitar made of a combination of Rosewood from Brazil for the back; European spruce for the top, and a Spanish cedar for the neck. He took the instrument, ranged the strings and smiled with satisfaction. *"You've saved me in so many ways!"* Suddenly, he was engaged in an old tune;

"I fly a starship,

Across the Universe divide,
and when I reach the other side,
I'll find a place to rest."

"Hey, Pavarotti," a high voice came out from a microphone placed in his suit. "The shuttle is about to exit."

"Tell them to wait!"

"You only have a few minutes to board."

Leo returned his guitar to its case.

"Andrew…."

"What?"

"Make sure the ships reach their destination," Leo urged.

"You know I will."

"Hey! I love you, man."

"I love you too, be safe."

With shaking hands, he took a piece of paper and wrote: *"To Jacob."* The young man had shown skills with instruments and enthusiasm for music. He surely would appreciate the detail. Leo stepped out of his room and ran through the corridor. There was no time for anything else. With quick steps, he jumped into an elevator. *"This would be a decent end,"* his pulse accelerated. *"No time to write memoirs,"* he thought.

Leonardo King Baylor was often misjudged. He was recognized as a wealthy eccentric man, although the "sensible critic" considered him brilliant and visionary. Others found him horrible tenacious, and bold. A man owner of a passionate spirit. Even his enemies couldn't deny, that a sophisticated worldly air around him made everyone feel special.

The truth was that he drove on contention, and he was best when his adrenaline boiled. His tired gaze still retained vivid flashes of his intense life. *"I'm thankful for this day."*

He was relieved- *"My life was blessed and worth telling. But what story is not magnificent, however brief? Life is a miracle."* *He thought.*

And death was no mystery to him. Mr. Baylor knew, without a doubt, what comes after the tragic end, as he saw too many die. "Tangle Destinies," that was he called the angel of death.

"Not all of us end in the Heavens, that's for sure." He said, as he waited for the elevator, he convinced himself that he was not escaping Earth and the horrors occurring on the planet, but just completing his latest mission.

He was excited at the thought of reaching the end of his long existence, but he did not realize that the most intense memories would hit his head, making his mission painful.

In an instant, he was plunged back in time. Then, as the elevator moved quickly, he vividly remembered the day his life changed forever. The day he turned seventeen.

Two

May of 1396
Castle in Norland

Enigma

The day his life changed, Leo was galloping at full speed with the wind in his face. He could see the ruby glow of torches shone on the dark castle, at a distance. He was heading back home, and the year was 1396. The north wind brought him a soft breeze that refreshed his sweaty body and his tormented spirit. He knew his father; King Philippe was overwhelmed, probably furious against him.

"Has he been found yet?" The King asked impatiently to his servants back in the castle.

"Yes, my lord. He was drinking in the town tavern with peasants," answered his servant, Martin. "He was told to return at once, your majesty."

The old monarch stopped, grabbed Martin's by the shoulders, and yelled, "Drinking with peasants, you said? There is not a drop of honor in the imprudent brute!" The sovereign shoved the little man and pushed him to the other side of the wall. "Instruct Andrew to prepare the prince for the ceremony at his arrival."

"Yes, your majesty," the servant bowed.

"Now, go. Move!" Said the worried father, disappearing through a massive oak door, leading to a hall followed by his personal guards.

The Kingdom of Norland stood firm amongst the lands of the west. A small nation with legendary war leaders. Warriors and heroes with strategic skills that brought prosperity to the island. In the distance, the careless figure of the prince appeared on the horizon, riding his fine steed.

"There is a big agitation for your welfare, my lord," said the footman, receiving Leo.

"I'm to blame, Willard." The prince looked buzzed. "Inform the King that I'm confined, so he can proceed with his torture," affirmed the heir to the throne, taking off his cape. Leo had an attractive complexion; he was tall, pale, and handsome. His full lips accentuated his sharp eyes, which were gray and splattered with tones of dark blue, ready to explore anyone and anything. Nevertheless, he was owner of a majestic personality, the young prince was cast down on his 17 birthday. The expectation and general excitement didn't match his indifference.

"My lord, you shall get ready for tonight," suggested Willard to the prince who was running careless among cooks and servants that diligently worked the entire day.

"Don't bother me now," he answered with disdain.

The banquet was elegantly displayed on burly oak tables, adorning the reception hall. It was easy to detect the aroma of freshly baked bread. Leonard took a quick look at the feast. A variety of delicacies; poultry, succulent pork stuffed with fruits and nuts. Large cuts of meat, imported wines, and exotic desserts were prepared for the occasion. A large group of servants was busy decorating with fresh fruits and flowers.

"My lord," exclaimed the butler on seeing his master. The servants froze and bowed.

"Don't mind me. Continue your task. Everything looks splendid, except me," said the prince sarcastically, running to his chamber. While climbing the stairs he cursed his fortune. For years the kingdom was under the shadow of the black plague. The terrible epidemic took the lives of almost half of the kingdom. After helping her subjects for months, his mother, the Queen fell victim of the fatal disease. Prince Leonard was only ten years old when he attended his mother's funeral.

After the funeral, the boy who was once an active and smart became an odd teenager, wandering lonely in the castle chambers for weeks, while his father failed to keep himself sober. Soon, the prince lost interest in his studies. He was constantly bored, overwhelmed, and sleepy during lessons. In addition, Leo's annoying attitude irritated his tutors to the point of desertion. Fortunately for the boy, Lord McAssey, an enthusiastic and persuasive teacher, convinced King Phillipe to introduce his son to music.

"By teaching him an instrument, we might bring the prince back to the world," said McAssey to the King, praying for a miracle.

"My child has become difficult to educate and love," answered his majesty skeptically.

"He's not a child anymore, my lord. But a young man with a lonely heart," said Lord McAssey. Yet, surprisingly, Leo reacted positively to his educator, who helped him heal his mourning and regain his concentration.

Once inside his chamber, the prince ordered everyone to leave the room, as he sank down on a purple loveseat. After heavily drinking in the tavern, his stomach turned over, and he found impossible the idea of becoming King in the next few hours. He took a deep breath, got up, and tried to open the window, as he gazed at a stained glass long and narrow, tempting him to escape but making it utterly impossible. The temperature dropped, and the dark sky foretold rain. Finally, he could open the latch to breathe. The aroma of fresh pines went to his lungs and calmed his anxiety. An impossible memory crossed his mind. He remembered his father's discussion, the morning before.

"When one has not had a good father,
one must create one."
- Friedrich Nietzsche

"I can't remember when I spoiled you so bad, that now you are afraid of becoming a man," King Phillipe said incredulously. He was sitting comfortably on an immense table, enjoying his breakfast.

"I beg your pardon, my lord?" The prince asked angrily from the other side of the table.

"You have come of age, Leonard," his father warned. King Philippe was similar in constitution to his son. He approached life with an easy vigor and a solid ceremonious character.

"Your subjects are loyal. They don't want a new King," said the prince with his distinct low voice.

"Indeed!"

"Why are you doing this to me? I don't want to take your place."

"I'm tired, son."

Leo walked towards his father and said, "and what is the purpose of this secret meeting prior to the coronation?" The young man inquired while holding an empty jug of wine, he picked up from the table.

"The purpose," the King took the jug back, "is to make sure that you are a worthy sovereign. This exercise is part of your education."

"If you insist."

"I do," he was chewing, "after your coronation, I want to retire to *Wenrial Château*."

"At BayCastle?"

"YES!"

"For an exile?"

"A retreat. This shall ease my mind," the King smiled, "I'll be available to you in a case of any substantial conflict or war."

"I see," Leonard was upset. He blushed angrily. "So be it…I've been alone all my life, this doesn't make any difference," he cried.

"I wish you stop the insolence, young man."

"And I wish you explain to me your bloody game, father."

"Sit," the old man ordered and tried to speak calmly.

"We both attended a pre-coronation ceremony."

"AND?"

"You will be presented with a series of questions, about your character. There is no need for you to answer them correctly because your interviewers will be able to perceive what truly lies in your heart."

The King could see the frustration on his son's face; he wasn't sure if a single word was getting through to the young man's brain. He paused, and took a deep breath.

"If you are not worthy, you will perish!"

Leo stood perplexed, "is this a buffoonery? I'm descendant of a sacred linage."

"True," the King replied, and cleaned his mouth. Next he addressed him with solemnity, "and you shall prove it, tonight."

Leo looked aggravated. His father ignored him and continued, "You must understand, your privileges are greater than just a kingdom and a fortune. We must assure that you are adequate for the responsibility, and it's sadly not entirely up to me." Finished the monarch sternly.

"I see…" Leo whispered, his thoughts miles away. He wasn't prepared to face extinction at the hand of a bunch of decaying medieval men. He felt adrenaline running through his head, his face flushed with fury. "Excuse me, my lord. I lost my appetite," Leo said and walked fast towards the door.

"You should take some fresh air. Ride your best horse into the woods."

"I will!" answered the prince feeling the urgency to disappear from the Earth.

The Alchemist

A burst of blue light was expelled from an old cottage located deep in the woods. Minutes later, three mysterious figures directed their steps towards an old carriage. Two young men were carrying boxes that looked like coffins. Suddenly, an older man appeared with a white beard and long hair, he held a golden goblet in his hands. "Hurry! I have to be present at the ceremony previous to the coronation. It is getting late."

Then, with incredible agility, they whinnied the horses, and took the road to the castle.

"How far is the Castle?" Asked the youngest.

"Not too far. We should arrive on time. I need to give the potion to the prince, or the arrangement would be a ruin," said a man in a white beard.

"No worries, the prophecy would be fulfilled!" Noticed the third wizard.

Back in his room, the prince continued glancing towards the front entrance. Large chariots were approaching the castle from a distance. *"They went as far as making sure the horse reins matched their laughably conceited transport,"* he sighed with a dreadfully smile. *"All of them are frivolous and pompous."* Once the chariots reached the castle the nobles started descending onto the path of the main gate. The prince looked at them with contempt. Each one of them, he'd known since childhood. The aristocrats were close to him all the time; their faces watching him, judged his every action, and performing all kind of intrigues against him.

The young man focused on a single chariot, which looked out of place; it was tatty, and straightforward, a bit rotten. Leo sat perplexed at the odd arrival, his eyes following it every inch up the castle gates, eager to satisfy his curiosity. Leo kept still as the stranger descended; as soon as his feet touched the ground the nobles around him huddled and stared at the atrocious man. Leo wished, he could hear what they were saying; he squinted to try to see the stranger's face, and sighed in frustration. The man jogged swiftly with his back towards the tower, and his hood on. He swore he had seen the man before, creeping around the castle. There was something about his walk, the way he pressed his fingertips together, one by one with an open palm, mania that the prince also had.

"Everything about him is so familiar, yet so creepy." Leo thought.

His sudden interest in the strange man sparked an almost child-like excitement. But all distracted, soon he completely forgot to get ready for the ceremony.

The Squire

Abruptly, the chamber doors opened, from them emerged, Andrew. A thin young man with an elegant posture, a soft voice and a distinctive manner of speaking, graceful and irreverent. Andrew was the prince's squire and longtime friend.

Leo looked at his servant with an air of disbelief.

"Ever heard of privacy?" he said, grabbing his guitar.

"Apologies for the interruption, but your father instructed me to clean your butt."

Leo sang merrily: "*He holds tears in his eye, and pain in his heart.*"

"Ah, splendid. You've been waiting for me!"

"I rather choose the gallows," he said, laying aside his lute.

Andrew was highly intuitive at predicting the prince's moods. Nobody else knew him as well. He walked across the room, and two servants followed him carrying buckets of boiling water.

"Your bath is ready. Hurry, the guests are arriving, my lord," he dismissed the servants. The prince sat into the bathtub and felt like he was literally being immersed into a soup, like a bird in a pot. Then, major suffering increased as Andrew soaped him roughly.

"Are they in the Great Hall?"

"Most of them."

"I wish I could disappeared. Melt in this water," he submerged.

Leo pictured all the elders waiting for him, drinking and laughing as he was served for the main course. "*Covey of swine.*" His thoughts were interrupted by a brutal splash of hot water.

"ANDREW, this is too hot!"

"Pardon me, I took the liberty of rescuing you from your tragic state," he said. The squire was two years his senior, and the only survivor of the black plague in his family. His biggest loss was his twin brother, Joshua who constantly appeared in his dreams. Cornelius, a good friend of the family connected to the service in the castle, rescued Andrew by sending him to serve the King. Leo and Andy hooked up when they met. In a few days, both kids developed a special bond with each other. The urgency of competition made them practice with swords and bows until nightfall. Together, they had fun exploring every room in the castle. Partners in crime of all kinds of trouble; they complicated the lives of the servants by hiding artifacts and spying on the maidens when they bathed in the streams of the forest. The prince never had so much fun with someone so delightful and easy going. Andrew felt admired and developed a protective instinct for the only person alive who had his affection.

Andrew threw a towel to Leo, "look what your father gave me."

He opened a large coffin. From it produced a feminine garment. A ceremonial robe.

"Magnificent gown!" Said the servant with faint sarcasm in his tone. The gown was a long full houppelande. Purple, heavily embroiled with silk and gold threads and flaring sleeves. "I understand it has been worn by your ancestors, both kings, and queens."

The prince glanced at it scornfully.

"The crown is simple gold with sapphires and rubies," noticed Andy, while he placed it on a red velvet pillow. "You should be eager to wear the crown of Norland," pointed the servant wearing the crown for a moment, looking at himself at a large mirror.

"Why? To become my father's puppet?" He asked somberly.

"You can't be serious!"

"Andrew, I don't want any of this."

"What do you mean? You will be the ruler of the land," he said while wearing the crown with pride.

"I drive my purpose to life delights without afflictions and good times," cried, Leo.

"There are not good times or bad times. There's only life. Cruel existence that we must endure," he answered in a bored tone, placing the crown back into the coffin.

"You know, this morning, I took a ride through the woods," said Leo with passion. "I recalled the simple joys of our childhood. Sweet memories of happy summer days." His eyes light up as emotions run through his body like a wave of energy. "There was an ecstasy, a delight to be alive, that cannot be compared to anything in the world."

Andrew got quiet, then he stared at the prince and asked. "I know you well. This nostalgia is … about your mother, isn't it?"

Leo hunched his shoulders, "I cannot forget as easily as you, I wish she'll be here today," he answered bitterly. "My drunk father could be the ruling king until he dies!" Exclaimed Leo.

"Stop the nonsense," replied Andrew. "You were born to be a king…our sovereign. It's normal to be nervous…"

"No!" Leo interrupted, but Andrew covered him with the gown. The prince took his head from it like a turtle, and said concerned. "I've noticed the comings and goings…They're planning a strategy."

"Are they, who? What can they do to you?"

"I don't know, a conspiracy."

"Oh, please."

"Maybe I have to fight for the throne, defeat a beast, or beat a warrior."

"No, no, you belong to a dynasty of kings, and you are next in line. It's your right to claim the throne."

"The Alchemist visited my father, several times."

"Oh, come on. That old fart. He has only been here once… yesterday!"

"He's evil and macabre."

Andrew held back a laugh, "You're not confident, you don't feel ready to rule…Is that so?"

"I'm not ready. I just want to have an ordinary life. Enjoy the delight of conquering every dream, travel freely to distant lands and… "

"And chase maidens," added the squired mockingly, while he was gathering his shoes.

"Right! Chase maidens," Leo finally smiled back.

Andrew finished the last touches on his master, and opened the door.

"Grow a pair, off you go!"

Crème de la Crème

When outside the chamber, his heart raced uncomfortably. His vacant gray eyes were fixated upon the floor he stepped on lightly. *"If my mother were here alive, things would be different."* He thought. Next, he headed down a narrow hall into the main room, and realized he was paying particularly attention to every detail of the castle. He took a glance at the gray stone walls. They were always so cold and meticulously decorated with pride items; embroiled crests, tapestries, portraits, and memories of the Holy War.

"After this madness, I shall not allow my father to drive me into an arranged marriage. This, I swear!" He assured, standing next to his ancestor's portraits.   He swiftly made his way to the throne room, and into the reception hall. The rest of the castle seemed sad compared to this scene. He could barely make his way through the crowd of servants, hustling through the tables. The prince took a rapid look at the King's throne room. The throne of his father proudly claimed the center of the room - a stunning piece carved of marble and confected with gold. Above the throne flew the kingdom banner - a gold lion confronting a crimson dragon. Gold and red drapes hung from the tall stone walls. He stopped

next to steps. A fake wall camouflaged him. Leo could observe the nobles, without them noticing. Members of the court and their families. All dressed elegantly. The young man could feel their judgmental stares. Musicians were eagerly performing over a loud wave of conversation. He saw the Campbell's a feudal family, and their two daughters sitting in the center trying to attract attention. Surrounded by men was Errol, the despicable Lord of Bremen, taking loudly about gold and property. They all babbled over one another as if their conversation was the most worthy of listening. Suddenly, Leo entered the room. Everybody froze at the sight of the prince and greeted him bowing. The young heir couldn't endure so much hypocrisy, he knew them well. All were aristocrats obsessed with power. Fond of intrigues and secret manipulation.

Willing to do anything to win the King's favor. Maybe the wise thing to do was to amuse himself with them and flip the game board from time to time, just for fun. The prince saluted them and continued through a corridor disappearing followed by murmurs and giggles.

"So handsome!" A female murmur crossed the walls, and the prince managed to hear it, gaining confidence. The pre-coronation ceremony would be held in a private lounge- an ancient room at the end of the main hall. The room would be full of wise men, priests, and the Alchemist. A wizard of an infamous reputation. In an instant, Leonard turned out facing the edge of the lounge. He was standing in front of a wood door, next to his father.

Three

Conspiracy

"It is time, son," said King Phillipe with a formal tone.

"I'm ready."

"Splendid."

A large rusted door opened, the air was saturated with a musty odor. The room was full with men staring at the prince. A chilled wind could be detected, and fireplace was lit, filling the room with a golden light. In the center a big chair was empty, waiting for the new King.

"Inside, your highness," cried a deep voice. "We've been waiting for you."

The prince felt a chill running down his back, his hands were sweating. His father grabbed him by the arm as they walked inside the chamber. The men bowed at the sight of the royal heir. Most of the Lords highly disapproved of Leonard. They condemned the sudden affair as they were convinced that the prince wasn't ready to rule.

"Allow me, have a seat your graces," said Bartholomew, the Bishop of Kennot, who was heading the board. He was a tall man, with a bulky complexion, grey hair, and a white beard- a wealthy man who accumulated a fortune from trading. The prince bowled back and sat on the throne prepared for him.

"We shall commence." The Bishop approached him, "Leonard, from the House of Baycastle, and from the line of the defenders of the Faith." He called him. "On your knees, my lord for your initiation." The Bishop placed a small purple cushion at the prince's feet and continued.

"Tonight, you will be proclaimed sovereign of our nation. We desire that you conceive the wisdom of the words that would be spoken. Secret knowledge passed from generation to generation, with no better intention than fulfill your life with happiness and prosperity.

Therefore, open your heart and mind to them. Embrace them and receive them, as your ancestors did. In the name of the Father, The Son, and The Holy Spirit, Amen!" He showered him with holy water.

"It is required that your grace drinks a potion specially prepared for this occasion," instructed the priest. "After the potion is completely consumed, I'll proceed with the ceremony," he added firmly. The priest swiftly moved towards the center of the room, where a small table was placed. On the table sat vial containing a dense greenish substance. Leo felt immediately disgusted when he saw the potion, then the priest held the glass and poured a generous amount in a golden goblet, adorned with stones. The Alchemist, dressed in a colorful robe, stood up, reached the throne, and offered the goblet to the young man. Leo dared to stare at him. The old man had penetrating eyes, and with a grim smile, he approached the prince. A strong smell of eucalyptus and lavender enveloped the room. Leo hesitated for a few seconds before drinking the potion. He glazed at his father, who was trying to read his face. His father nodded as a sign of approval. Then, he trusted him completely, closed his eyes, and drank the entire sour potion. The prince felt dizzy and his stomach became upset. The Bishop stood up and addressed the crowded room.

"The responsibility of ruling this kingdom will fall on your shoulders. To accept such great privilege, you must demonstrate your value and be loyal to your duty."

The Bishop continued with a book on his right hand, "for that purpose," he took a deep breath. "Seven tokens will be presented to you during this ceremony. Lord Darcy, please..."- Announced the priest, and pointed to the first speaker.

Revelation

A tall, blushed man stood up and made his way towards the throne to offer the first token- an onyx stone. Big as a buttercup,

"The first token refers to foods and beverages that nourish your body. This food and drinks only can be consumed to keep your body healthy and nourished. Remember that fasting for the body is food for the soul. So, when to feed or to drink are the only reasons for your existence, you will lose this token."

"I don't love food," the prince raised his shoulder, "food loves me. It's always in my mouth!"

"Your majesty during the section mockery wouldn't be tolerated, so binge not." So noticed the Bishop, who perceived Leo as an absent- minded rascal. The prince accepted the first token. A tall man approached him with flashy eyes and offered a second token- a small sparking emerald. "As the leader that you are, you will have busy days full of commitments. Whenever you have a task ready to expire, you will fulfill it until the end. Indolence shall not appear in your daily work. Although, you will have time to relax and sleep, or perform a pastime. You will always prioritize to your responsibility, and feel the joy of accomplishment. Languish not," he said and placed the emerald in the prince's hand. Leo played with the emerald for a minute while an old warrior approached him. He cleared his throat to call the young's man attention. Lexington was the warrior's name. He was a bulky man with a body covered with war scars. Honor and pride were in the house of Lexington for generations. The warrior dressed in a fur coat bent over and gave the young monarch a silver dagger adorned with shiny sapphires.

"Soon," he stated. "A sword as notable as; *Excalibur or Durendal* will be assigned to you. Because enemies you will have, although you don't want them. Even when you don't look for them, they will come to you, as envy domains the human heart. But your heart shall not be a prisoner of any hatred, for the opposite, you should be generous and always be glad about the success of your adversaries, so they turn into your alias. So envy, not." The statement puzzled the prince for a minute.

Next was the turn of the astrologist of the kingdom. A savvy old man who talked slow and stared at the prince. "By your lineage and noble birth, the gift of true love has been given to you at birth."

"I'm a blueblood prince," Leo said, smiling proudly.

"Allow me…. to continue, your majesty. True love will arrive in your life, filling a deep emptiness in your heart, at a precise time of a very lonely existence."

"Well said!" The rascal softly clapped.

"A helpless gap inside you will end forever, but you shall fight lust. Lust will be around you constantly as a temptation. The youngest and more beautiful creatures will surround you. The importance of your true love will be destroyed if you fall into temptation; however, your noble heart will help you to preserve this token, the ruby of Osiris."

"Ahhhh," the men echoed.

"Osiris, the stone of true love and passion. So Lust not."

Finally, the heir looked pleased with his collection. His stomach growled, his mind recalled the banquet outside. The King himself stood up and approached him.

"Good time to eat. This is over!" Leo thought.

"As sovereign that you will be," the King raised his voice. "You would never allow the loss of your common sense and let the anger dominate you. Major tasks would come. Your character would be tested like a piece of carbon that becomes a diamond by pure pressure. You can't lose the senses; you will raise your words, not your voice. Think before you act, use reason over instinct.

You shall be a successful negotiator and never allow the anger to control your mind. So rage not." King Phillipe opened his hand and presented his son with a diamond. Leo proudly grabbed the precious gem and stared at his audience.

The Archbishop approached him and gave him a carved box to place his tokens. "Exactly what I need, thank you."

"Precisely, my lord." The priest took a deep breath and continue. "You were born owner of immense wealth to benefit your subjects. So you would be able to extend your richness and distribute it to the poor and needy. But if your heart is moored off the possessions, and your mind looks for greed, then you will lose this token. He handed Leo a golden nugget. So covet not." Leo looked at the nugget with caution.

A monk emerged out of the shadows; it was a monk from lands of the far Orient. He dressed in black and orange robes, with no hair on his head. He approached the prince and dropped a small jade stone into his hand. He leaned over and spoke with a soft voice. "Boast not my child as pride is the seed of all evil. Pride corrupts all that it touches. Vainglory centers on self-sufficiency where there is no need of another man or even the supreme conscience." He paused, stared at the young man, then, added. "Be humble and moderate; as these are not weakness, but unique strengths. Your Grace's be confident yet never arrogant. Be open to learn from all men you will cross roads with, and be certain that everyone has a lesson to offer."

The members of the conclave remained solemn.

"When answers won't be found because you think you are too righteous, or your heart is full of pride. Step outside of your state and take a look at the stars in the vast sky, then." He paused. "Listen to nothing but the beat of your heart, belong. Let your mind, and spirit…be one with the cosmos!"

"What's a cosmos?" The young man asked, intrigued.

"The question your majesty is: What is not part of the Cosmos?"

A slight murmur covered the room. The prince was puzzled again.

"Remember, young man, the path of the true leader only can be walked by humble steps," and saying this, he vanished. Leo looked out for the monk, but instead, he saw his reflection on his father's crown. Then he thought. *"How can I be humble when I am so well equipped?"*

The King read his son's face. He blamed himself for the way the young man acted. Then, he stood up and addressed his son for a second time, cleared his throat and roared like a lion.

"What separates great rulers from the rest of the mankind; is the ability to do more."

"*When is this going to end*?" Leo whispered.

"Resist the distractions of your mind and center on the thing that matters most, be guided only by purpose." He took a deep breath and exclaimed, "More than becoming a successful king, I expect you to emerge as a man of great value."

Leonard became impatient.

"It is my desire that tonight! You will be transformed into an alpha male so your roar could be heard all over your kingdom!" His father raised his arms.

"Hail the King!" Men shouted with passion.

Leo looked at his father then said impatiently, "This stupid ritual is insane."

"OH!" The elderly disapproved of the disrespect.

"This medieval conjuration is OVER!" He stood up, shot down the tokens, and tried to reach the door.

The sinister Alchemist stood and shouted "STOP AT ONCE!" The wizard looked at him with eyes that dug into Leo's subconscious, paralyzing him for a moment. Then the vicious man approached with a goblet and offered him a second drink.

"My lord, do you understand that losing your tokens means losing your life?" Asked the wizard.

Leonard's knees were weak, and he caught himself wishing to disappear. Still he shouted back. "I shall not endure… this function is over! "Leo said and walked towards the exit. "MOVE!" Order the guards at the door. "I was born in a regal cradle, chosen by God's will to be King, and none will deprive me of my right born privilege."

All eyes looked at him with disapproval; King Philippe covered his forehead with his right hand showing shame.

"Coward!" Someone mumbled.

Whispers grew louder.

He was not a coward; the prince looked at his audience, trying to find the offender. He stared at the sorcerer, grabbed the goblet, and drank from it. The potion now was deep green and had a sour flavor. In a second, he felt sick and wanted to vomit. The Bishop stood up and proclaimed.

"We will proceed with the coronation ceremony in the main hall." He showed a large crucifix. "Defender of the Holy Church!"

A storm broke loose, and thunder could be heard.

Leo barely walked down. That had to be a bad joke. His legs were numb and his vision blurry, his heart started racing, and everything seemed to be happening in slow motion.

"Infamy, I've been poisoned!" The prince shouted. "Father, help me."

The Alchemist spoke.

"You have drunk a magic potion. If you keep your promise of virtue, you will retard the aging process. Now you will live a life of A THOUSAND YEARS."

Confusion was in everybody's eyes. Finally, a cry was produced from the back. "Witchcraft!"

"Ambrosia."Someone shouted.

"It's the Fountain of Youth."

"Antidote, give me an antidote, quick." Furious Leo charged his sword towards the potion maker.

"Leonard STOP at once." Yelled the King.

"Why you did this to me? He cried. "ANSWER ME, FATHER, I'M YOUR ONLY SON!" He shouted and got dizzy. Life of a thousand year, had he heard right? He grabbed his father's robe while feeling a fire in his stomach. Perception of everything was vague and confusing. Bells were tolling, matching the beats of his heart. Horrified, the prince pulled out his sword, and without thought cut a straight line across his palm. A millennial man could not afford to bleed to death. After all, this would assure him, he had closed no deal with madmen. With terror in his eyes, he witnessed his immediate recovery. His hand healed instantly, leaving nothing but only the mark of fresh blood. Leo stared at the audience, who looked at him horrified.

As if summoned, fanfares announced the beginning of the festivities, the Coronation Ceremony.

"Hail the King!" Someone shouted in the back to the confused men. Phillip repeated with a trembling voice, "Hail the King" when the huge pair of oak doors opened and filled the room with blinding lights from the main hall. Leo dropped his sword and faced the crowd, astonished. They were waiting impatiently to see him wearing the crown. His face was pale. Destiny caught up with him. Now, he had to be a man. He was their sovereign and ruler.

"You are not a drop of the ocean,
You are the entire Ocen in a drop."
Rumi.

 Four

Navigator Starship:
Warrior I-Cosmos 24x-Infinity

Paradigm

Rapid steps lead Mr. Baylor to the main transport tube; a small crystal door opened to reveal a tiny entry. He lowered his head and sat in the enclosed space. Then, carefully, he placed his helmet next to a robot who greeted him coldly, "Good Afternoon, Mr. Baylor."

"Yes," Leo smiled while taking off his gloves.

"Getting ready for launching?"

"Ready…tin man," Leo adjusted his hearing aid, and noticed his right eye withered, but the most severe damage was to his knees witch he refused to replace with bionic parts.

"Is everything OK?" Asked the android while Leo rubbed his knees.

"Don't grow old, robot."

"I will not, sir. I'm a piece of fine technology."

"Me too. The difference is that I have free will and you don't, and I pay the price with a mortal body."

"Can you explain?"

"Blow a fuse!" he answered while memories of one of the most horrible battles came to mind.

"Blow a fuse? I can't damage myself, or anybody else, Mr. Baylor."

"Of course not. You're not human."

"Five minutes to board." The Android announced, faking a smile.

The horizontal elevator accelerated and for the first time in many years, Leo felt a cold shiver down his spine... *Fear, anxiety? It felt foreign.*

After his coronation, Baylor fought terrible battles to control his constant mood change. Depressions and anxieties took him a prisoner of his mind, until he accepted the reality of the material world. The state of total peace is reserved for the dead.

A discomfort grew in the pit of his stomach until he could no longer shrug it off, "No, I'm not afraid of dying." He murmured.

"Repeat," asked the robot.

"Nothing, let's board the shuttle." He answered as images of his past were alive back in his memory. Fresh as the blood stains that mixed with mud and snow during a battle. It was a winter night on the battlefield of Bridgestone. The year was 1421, or maybe 1441 - he wasn't sure. What was vivid in his brain was the deep feeling of frustration and anger he felt that night. Soon, he was transported in time, and for a few seconds, he could feel the cold wind blowing, as he walked carefully among his defeated army. Blood, pain, and death asphyxiated the senses. His eyes were directed to the vanishing horizon. Yet somehow, he still managed to make his way across the field through the corpses.

An enormous moon cast shadows over the frozen emerald grass. Above, the sky was filled with a beautiful display of stars and celestial lights of violet and bluish hues. Below the snow covered ground in white and splashes of crimson. Blood of his army mixing with enemy's corpse. He stopped and scanned the field, moved by adrenaline, paralyzed by fear. He only could see dead and defeat. Old and young men alike required shelter; some wounded, some in agony, some dead. Though he was trolling, his heart was racing, his pupils dilated.

"We won't bow to a tyrant!" Cried Leo to one of his captains. The men stopped at a blooded pond; a horse was dying.

"Milord, this destruction cannot mean so little" Said Captain Edward. "We have to face it...we are defeated," roared the captain.

"No! This is not over," cried the King walking fast to the camp.

Everything was disturbingly still, then out of the corner of his eye, he saw it again. Yes, it was a shadow, maybe a spy. Anyway, the thing was following him during the battle. Probably was nothing. Or maybe was the angel of death.

Earlier that day, the sun was setting over the camp of King Leonard's armies. Warriors were busy burying the dead and nursing the wounded. The rest of the army rested or tended their horses. Towards the back of the camp was a black and silver tent where Leonard was pacing, puzzled like a caged tiger. For the first time in years, he was ill and insecure. Nevertheless, he stood in his tent with three of his most trusted warriors.

"What is your report?" Leo asked one of his men.

They all stood silent, clearly feeling low-spirited after an all-out fight.

"We fought without victory." Said ill at ease, Sir Konan of Thoannon -the most physically agile warrior. He stood over six feet tall, with huge muscles and the strength of a bear. The rest of the warriors stared at each other. Edward was the highest-ranking knight of Norland. He was inches shorter than Konan, and although he was certainly no match. Edward was well known for his talent for strategy.

The last Knight, Sir Tybalt of Eagan, was the most inexperienced of the group; however, he had won a unique ranking in the king's army. He had a natural flair with the bow and arrow, born a commoner; he shocked hundreds of people at a tournament when he proved to be the challenger with a perfect aim. Emerging a victorious champion, Leo decided to find a way to make Tybalt's natural gift a perfect weapon.

Captain Edward considered himself the leader of the group so, he dared to break the silence, "I am not optimistic, milord," his voice worried, his spirt hopeless. "We've lost many men. We have many injured, sorely wounded. The enemy's army doubles ours in numbers." The King was listening carefully, his eyes narrowed.

Bruises and scrapes were visible on his warriors. Leonard was wounded and bleeding from his left shoulder, "I refuse to give up our freedom. We will fight until the last man. Victory is possible. This is not our first battle!" The King inquired.

"No! Milord, but it can be our last. We knew we were outnumbered," replied the captain with indignation. "We are at a disadvantage since they were marching from the west with the setting sun behind them."

"Are you predicting our defeat?"

"I am afraid so…" Edward clasped his helmet next to his chest, "you are only delaying the inevitable."

"No! We are not defeated," Leo shouted, pacing around the tent with an air of disapproval.

"Milord!" Sir Konnan raised his voice in despair, "my men are tired and hungry. We haven't rested for days. We don't have enough supplies…and…"

"I know, I know." The King interrupted. He couldn't hear more. Tremendous frustration showed on their faces. Optimism had no room in their hearts. Sir Tybalt looked honestly at the King then added- "Milord, we've to prepare…for the outcome."

Leonard replied by making a hand gesture. He looked at his men eager for a sign of hope, but he only saw fear and disappointment, then he exclaimed. "Order your men to return to their tents in the camp- try to rest; I will call you if I need you."

The knights bowed and left him alone. He sat down on a chair; he became aware of a pain in his shoulder. He was bleeding, and his left hand was shaking.

Five

ndrew stood at the edge of the tent. "Permission to enter, Milord,"

"Permission, granted."

"Gracious, gracious, Lord," replied the servant who kept his master under his eye for safety.

"Like you even care…"

"I still ought to ask, allow me," he said while taking Leonard's armor. "I understand; today's battle was difficult," the servant noticed awkwardly as he used a rag to clean his master's wound.

"It was a humiliating defeat," answered his friend. "The enemy obliterated us; we are losing more men by the hour. Most of them are deadly injured."

Andrew looked into Leonard's eyes; it deeply troubled him to see his friend crestfallen. Over many decades, Leo gained the strength and experience to become a skillful warrior. He led his armies into numerous battles, many at his father's side. However, Leonard puzzled his soldiers as his appearance didn't change since his coronation. Although several years had passed, he had the looks of a man in his early twenties.

For the young sovereign, a year calendar was equivalent of an average between twelve for the rest of the people.

"I remember my first battle, Andrew," Leo said, opening a bottle of wine with his mouth, while his servant was cleaning his wound.

"A wave of angst paralyzed my body. I remember reaching for my father's face," he looked weary. "Then it happened, after the first wounded, nothing stopped me. I live to fight."

"Glory days of legendry battles, Milord!"

Leonard built a legendary reputation of damned and bewitched; many feared him, while others craved his head as a collectible trophy.

His servant was listening thoughtfully, watching amazed the prompt healing of the deep wound, which almost touched the bone.

"You have conquered victory before," said Andrew proudly.

"And a multitude of enemies," Leonard drank directly from the bottle -"My kingdom has become a coveted prize!"

"Envy is a passionate flattery. A strange combination of affection and hatred."

Leo bent down to remove his boots, and Andrew hurried back after emptying a bowl full of wet rags, "Allow me, milord, I'm finishing your shoulder with some bandages."

The king made a sign, "Never mind, it is only a scratch," and he placed some wine in his open wound, then with a gesture took a rag and bandaged himself. "Go and rest, I'll call you if I need you."

Andrew left in silence feeling his friend's sorrow. He hurried to his tent. As he walked through a narrow pad, he caught himself thinking about the day his life took a 90-degree turn.

Rage

Days after the uncommon coronation ceremony, Andrew noticed his friend's attitude decline in a spiral.

The new king would be moody, stay in bed for hours. Or walked outside and stared into the distance completely motionless, becoming irate about any topic.

"What happened to him? ...This new man I don't know." Andrew thought. But one morning, Leo confessed to his friend.

"Do you know what the problem is?" The young King said practicing with swords and shields with Andrew.

"No, what's the trouble, Milord."

"Nobody even stopped to think what I reckoned about this cursed life…" Leo hit his friend's shield with extraordinary rage.

"Hey!"-Andrew was defensive.

"The bastards…."-The monarch continued fighting passionately.

"What…what they did to you?"

"They went on….and on….for hours. Until they made me drink the damn potion." He growled and scratched Andrew's arm.

"What potion?"

"Do you dare to know?"

"Yes! Speak."

"I made a pact with Satan. Now you know!" Leo yelled with frustration. Tossed the sword and shield to the grown and headed to the castle.

After drinking some scotch, he finally opened his heart to his friend. Told him in detail all the events; explaining the secret meeting, the elders, the Alchemist. His promise to remain virtuous, and his thousand-year sentence. His friend listened carefully. He was incredulous. Andrew was well acquainted with the harshness of life. So, he decided to take action into his own hands and help his friend; he had to find the damn wizard to revert the spell.

On that same day, the sun was setting over the castle. Leo's father had been enjoying needed leisure after the recent coronation of his son, during which he learned the troubling news.

"We had been monitoring these spies for days, your majesty," said his captain, "we think, there's a plan to overthrow your rule. The Alchemist is involved."

Philippe felt his blood boil with anger; how could he have been so stupid and listened to the damn wizard. Phillip had to solve the treason and kill the Alchemist. So, he ventured deep into the forest without his guard. As he reached the famous skull hill, he noticed smoke from the east, definitely the place he sought. Upon arriving at the hut, he dismounted. Then, silently, approached it wearing a black hood of his cloak; he heard voices.

"I demand you give me the potion." Said a quivering voice.

"I warn you, risk not your life, milord." Said a dark, ghostly voice, unmistakably the Alchemist's, King Phillipe thought.

"You won't see another dawn, you fool!" Claimed the familiar voice with fear in its tone. Phillipe moved over and peeked in a wall crack. The scene was most unusual. Leonard's personal servant Andrew, was standing in front of the wizard, trapping him between a wall and a long sword, which he held firm with both hands, possibly because he wasn't strong enough to hold it.

"The only bloody fool is you!" Answered the wizard. "Just realize what you speak of magic potions and immortal kings… Nonsense!" The sorcerer said, spitting on the ground.

"You have some nerve threatening an old man!" Having said this, the Alchemist clapped his hands, and a dense blue smoke appeared from nowhere. The wizard knocked down Andrew's sword and made a run for it- at that moment, the old king kicked the door open just in time; and the Alchemist struggled to lose the king's grip. Then, the wizard stabbed the king with the sword. Immediately, Andrew picked up a giant vase and smashed it against the wizard's head, who fell to the ground.

The servant ran to the king's aid. "Milord, have you been wounded?"

Phillip growled and pointed to his side; his robe had a crimson stain that was starting to increase in size. Andrew looked frantically around the hut -if the sorcerer also wanted to live as long as Leo, he would have to make the potion.

Andrew blabbered while desperately looking for the miracle remedy. Finally, he stood and shuffled through the things the old wizard had in his cabin trying to find something regarding this eternal life tonic.

"Your majesty," he asked. "Is there anything you might know, anything about this potion?"

The old king laying on the ground tried to sit up against a stack of heavy crates. He'd been drinking all day, and his vision was blurry.

"No, I am afraid I cannot be of help." He said, shaking. His left hand was pressing on the wound firmly with a silk cloth. He tried to recall the conversations, anything the evil man may have given away about the potion. Then, suddenly, he told Andrew, "yes, he blabbered about having the ceremony at a specific time…when the moon…AH!."

The pain was increasing, "I believe it had something to do with the moon." The king became pail, "he used belladonna sprouts, and…"

"He would have to be making it right now!" Andrew leaped across the hut and looked inside a cauldron; it was sitting over the stove. The green thick liquid substance boiled ominously. He stared at it. Sweat dripped on his face.

"This shall be it! Your majesty, is this the potion?"

"I don't know," answered the old man, ready to faint.

Andrew wondered if the alchemist finished the potion, he dared not to add anything else, but he had no guarantee it would be safe to take it.

He took a look at the king, his clothes now completely drenched. There was no more time, so he grabbed a bowl and scooped a generous amount.

"You must drink this," he whispered.

"No, I deserve to die."

"Here, drink... You can't leave your son alone."

"I'm a bloody drunk. He's been alone all his life," Philippe claimed flooded with guilt.

"You're his guidance."

"No. He's all right ...he doesn't need me anyone," He coughed.

"Then, damn it all, curse him again."

The king took the servant by his lapel and roared, "he is my blood. You fool!"

Andrew offered the potion. Phillipe took a sip and confessed: "The wizard lied to me. He ticked me, Leonard needs to know." The squire nodded and also drank the potion. Andrew realized that father and son had being deceived, and someday, somehow they need to regain their confidence for each other.

 # Six

"Only the dead have seen the end of the war"
Plato

Back in the tent, the wind was blowing, and the brutal cold made the bones ache. As soon as Andrew left, Leonard felt a heavy aura of pessimism. It was the first time in decades that insecurity filled his heart.

This was not his first battle but could be the last one.

"What's happening to me? I can't see beyond this night."

He was a warrior king. The conflict of the war was significant and necessary in his times.

The battle was an imminent evil that made his blood burn with an internal fire. He felt passion and urgency to subjugate the enemy.

To see the blood of the wicked run like rivers in the conquered land, and define his kingdom. His frenetic urgency was to expand, to enslave the enemy and show him a fear never known. That was his destiny and glory. But that dark night challenged his courage. That night, the shadows turned his fierce spirit into horrible doubts. Overwhelmed by negative thoughts, he stood up in a quick motion and walked outside the tent on sore legs.

The sky was consumed by velvet darkness. Leo felt the cold wispy air predicting a massive defeat. His legs were weak, and the ground beneath them felt like quicksand. He sat on the cold grass, and looked at the multicolored firmament above him. So promising and peaceful. He had become fond of the idea that spirits floated around like celestial bodies, after death, forever. In perfect harmony. The memory of his mother got him. *"I am sure she is alive, maybe in one of the brightest shining stars."* -as soon as he visualized the image of his mother. He felt a strong surge of energy pulling him to the ground, his back touched the cold grass, and he could smell the fresh dew.

He felt like he was being pulled apart from his body. By instinct, he closed his eyes.

Then as intense as the cold in his face, he regressed to his early childhood. The image of his mother was painted in his mind like a projection, her abundant ruddy hair, her ivory skin. Her smile, was so warm, that it could bring a moment of happiness to the most bitter of man. Her voice, softly calling his name.

"L e o n a r d." He struggled to rise on his infant's legs. Her voice called him like a bee to the summer bloom. When he finally reached her arms. Sweet love embraced him. He was peacefully flooded. She was alive again. Suddenly, grey clouds darkened the stars; thunder could be heard in the distance. When he looked up, the image of his mother was gone. He jumped up, and now a black hooded figure was in front of him, staring at him with flashy eyes. It was the ultimate serial killer, dressed in a black robe holding a scythe, standing on a pile of skulls. It had to be the angel of the dead, collecting souls, ending his life. Suddenly, the earth rumbled by a high-pitched scream that sounded prominent from hell itself.

Leo swayed but managed to keep his feet on the ground. A lightning bolt hit near his feet. He froze for a second. The dark angel was gone, and decomposing bodies of the enemy soldiers were coming out of their graves and moving towards him. It felt like he had been knocked backward, his chest was aching, and his vision was blurred. A second lightning bolt showed the corps of soldiers closer to him.

"What's happening? This cannot be…unless, I'm dead too. But when, how I died?"-he thought. The human remains were anxiously looking for him. Revenge was the only emotion reflected on those bodies with putrefied flesh hanging on them. They were walking dead. A mighty howl covered the night, and Leo finally faced the creature following him during the day. A gigantic beast jumped, like it, fell from the sky. An animal the size of a bear, on all fours, like an enormous black dog.

"NO, I'm not dead!"-Leo shouted and ran to the woods, but the thing started chasing him with fangs long and threatening. Leo ran faster,

and the beast charged towards him with rage. Then, in a rush of instinct the young man sprung from the ground and started sprinting downhill. It sped up with ease in an almost unearthly way and attacked the king with a leap. Leonard was scared; he barely registered rolling towards the edge of a ravine. He dived into the river, hoping that he could make a quick getaway, but immediately regretted his decision; the river's current was unexpectedly strong, and it pulled him towards the bottom.

He struggled to get out without success until he was washed out at the entrance of what looked like a small cave. Leo heard the beast howl in the distance, and ran to the cave to hide.

Darkness

The entrance of the cave was modest.

The young man continued down a narrow space that kept getting smaller and smaller. A faint smell of sulfur emerged from the other side of the tunnel. Eventually, he had to get to his knees and crawl. The humidity was denser. There was water leaking off the walls. He almost was face down, when he felt a draft of cold air. The king continued to drag himself with his arms and tried to escape from whenever the air- stream was coming. Finally, he fell onto a stone. The place was dark and gloomy.

"UGH"- He grunted with pain; his shoulder was bleeding again.

"Ugh ugh ugh…" The echo of his voice reached him, and he suddenly visualized the place he was in; water could be heard dripping rhythmically in the distance.

A single thin ray of light came from above, presumably from the moon. It felt quiet, dark, and endless. An enormous space completely engulfed in darkness. Leo got up from the ground and walked towards the ray of light, shook his clothes, and tried to see how high the hole above was, but the beast was in front of him, the monster sprinted across the silver ray of moon. Leo was paralyzed.

"Who are you?" The young warrior called out, and he was afraid of the answer. The worst thing he could imagine was an encounter with the evil man, the Alchemist. A cloud covered the moon and he could not see anymore. Suddenly, the temperature in the cave increased; drops of sweat began to roll down his face. He tried to move, but his legs were not responding. His feet were planted upon the cave floor and would not yield.

The sulfur smell became so pungent, that made his eyes burn. The blue light turned purple, and diabolic patterns emerged from it. Leo was mesmerized by their effect, his legs finally obeyed, but he realized he could barely move.

It took him a second to realize that he was ankle deep in mountains of excrement, and from it, weird creatures that he assumed were earthworms started to crawl his legs.

"Where am I?" He asked and tried to see through the shadows. He could feel someone breathing….too close. His heart pumped so strong that he felt every palpitation.

"Answer me, who are you?"

A beast was visible again right before his eyes.

Almost as a reflection, Leo drew his sword, wounding him. The animal snarled such a force that he caused an earthquake, an avalanche of stones came from everywhere. The cave walls cracked, forming an alley, wide enough for Leo to jump on it and run away. Soon he was running in a corridor humid and hot as his boiling blood, and from the cracked walls, cries of pain could be heard. Leo didn't look back, but all his body was invaded by deep hatred.

Horrendous darkness and wickedness covered the place as he had never experienced before. At this moment, he concentrated all his energy on escaping the illusion, he could see the alley coming to an end.

"Hell…I'm in hell!" He exclaimed in panic- as he stopped abruptly. He was correct; the scene in front of him was dreadful. His face was covered with sweat- his body was soaking wet. He tried to turn back, but the walls moved and fell apart like sugar in his hands-"Charcoal?….. I know this place!"

A bunch of bats flew over his head. The cavern trembled, the road in his back closed completely –"NO!" He shouted. There was no option but to walk ahead to the burning space before his eyes.

"I'm in the afterworld," he mumbled, drying sweat from his face, clearing his view- "I'm dead…somebody killed me…and this is hell!" He said convinced.

Seven

Feeding the Beast

The open space before his eyes was unbelievable. It seemed eternally vast. Illuminated in shades of blood and fire. With boiling rivers of lava coming from the walls to a center on a burning lake. Faceless horrors attempted to escape the fiery lava. Their chilling shrieks echoed against the cavernous walls. The walking dead stepped slowly, losing their extremities and flesh towards the fire.

They melted in agony. Toxic air covered all. The earth trembled, and with a jump, the beast appeared in front of him, once more.

"FRIGHTENED?" -this time, the monster inquired in a deep voice inside Leonard's head. Now the young king was able to see him face to face. The enormous thing was a hideous demon, mocking him with a loud laugh. Leo noticed, he was feeding the beast with his fear, as the demon increased in size.

"I AM NOT FRIGHTENED!" Leo finally reacted and shouted with rage, as he fought the monster. The demon had the force of thunder, took Leo by the shoulders, and threw him into the lava, but he reached the edge of a rock, to avoid being swallowed by the boiling liquid. He looked down, and saw thousands of faces melting in deep sorrow. The demon lunged back, but Leo jumped to the ground, reached his sword, and cut one of the demon legs -the beast fell roaring. Next, the King jumped holding his sword with both hands and nailed it into the demon's heart, then kicked him into the lava. The beast disappeared slowly, burning every inch. A cloud of sulfur rose, Leo was unable to breathe, his eyes were irritated- his shoulder was bleeding again. He surrendered to an imminent death and prayed for a miracle, *"Almighty, most holy, and supreme, have mercy of my soul,"* he opened his eyes.

To his surprise, he gradually regained his breath, and solid surface was under his feet once more. Everything was dark, ashes were floating in the air resembling butterflies.

Private Inferno

"Where am I?

"Have you forgotten, Leonard, have you forgotten all?" Asked the silky voice.

"What?" It was too dark, he couldn't see. No, actually, he became blind. He panicked, he was in hell and that had to be Satan. "Go ahead kill me. Or I kill myself!"

"And allow your pain to win this battle?" The silky voice sounded wise and firm. It couldn't be Satan. Still, he was in despair. "Give me back my sight, stop my pain."

"All the leaving things cope with pain, fear, danger. The strongest survive."

"Why? Why does it have to be that way? Why do you hurt?"

"Only what you allowed to hurt you -will harm you."

Leonard was listening; he wanted to understand.

"Why I cannot see?"

"Fear blinds."

Leo nodded his head. "*This is not real…come one be still, this is not real.*"

"The fundamental is invisible for a heart wounded by doubts."

"Give me back my sight, I ask." Leo cried raising his arms, "I fear you not!" Tremendous anger invaded him. For a moment, he thought this was the game of the Alchemist.

"You are worse than a blind man." The stranger continued, "You allowed evil voices own you will."

"What do you want?" Leo was walking, touching the walls; his throat was dry.

The voice continued, talking inside his head, "I can feel your anxiety."

Leonard covered his ears, but it was useless. "*Be still, be still. I'm dreaming*" – he repeated to himself, but the voice continued inside his head. "You allowed negative thoughts, thoughts of poverty. Fears of forfeit."

Suddenly, the voice was reveling his deepest secrets, "you think you may not be able to produce an heir. Never being loved, and not being able to prevail in this dark era," Leonard shook his head.

"Leonard," the voice rumbled thru the cave, "didn't David defeat Goliath with a sling?"

"So, the legend tells."

"A young shepherd with nothing but a brave heart. He had faith."

Leonard felt pressure over his body. Then, finally he dared to shout.

"Yes! I have doubts… I DON'T BELIEVE!" -he fell on his knees. "I *don't believe, I don't believe…believe.*" –words echoed in the cave.

 # Eight

Pandemonium

"**W**hy not believe?" The wise voice asked.

"I rather hope not. Reality is what matters."

The King recovered his sight. A man dressed in a glowing white robe was next to him, and asked -"Then what is real?" Reality for you is only the perception of your senses. Can you trust your senses?"

"Yes!"

A soon as, he answered, there was a thud on the roof, the walls parted, and he sputtered out into the sky like a cannonball.

"And can you recognize the supreme conscious?"

"What?" -the young warrior didn't understand, but when in space, his body floated lightly. Suddenly, a blue light covered him and transported him like an elevator -he was inside of a gelatin bubble. He felt a chilly cold witnessing Galaxies crashed in front of his eyes. Thousands of images passed showing him life on thousands of planets. He couldn't understand. Soon, everything stopped abruptly. Static, his body floated. He tried to think, to understand. Yet, his brain was numb. He didn't move for an instant, and let nothing to happen. A sense of peace mastered him completely. There was immense knowledge impossible to decode in his brain -supreme beauty invaded him. He was not sure, if he was alive or he was back inside his mother's womb. His heart burned with immense love. Leo closed his eyes, allowing tears of joy to run down his cheeks. The extreme emotion had left his entire body trembling. "Love exists," he exclaimed in ecstasy.

"Yes, it does!" The voice was inside his head softly. Fear is the common denominator in the fourth dimension, in the subconscious mind. But love, faith, hope, benevolence. Those are gifts from the supreme conscious."

"They are divine gifts." The young King answered and realized he was kneeling back on a solid surface, he reached for help and said, "I can't see my victory in this battle."

"Then, you're defeated."

"I don't want to lose."

"You know well that to manifest a reality, you have to believe, think and feel the victory, in every cell of your body, without any doubt and with a grateful heart full of love."

"Sure, love for your enemies" – he repeated, sarcastically.

"Why not? They have fears like you."

At that moment the cave was lit.

"Have you thought that all fears are common, and in times of uncertainty, you all share the same concerns?"

"No, why should I care about other's fears?" He got up.

"Why not?"

The man levitated and circled around Leo.

"Don't fear them, instead look at them with your heart, listen to them with your soul"- said the mysterious figure and millions of blackbirds rose over Leonard's head. The bird's eyes were full of rage and horror. Their voices were loud.

"I will die in this war. I can't get cured. I hate my life. Things only get worse. The crops would be ruined. I can't pay my debts. There's no love. I can't find a job. The black fever will kill us all. I want to die. There's no food. We're living in a dark era. THERE IS NO GOD!"

The man in the white robe moved his arm, and all birds disappeared.

"Worries, anxieties consume the divine flame of the soul!"

The words rumbled in Leo's brain. He felt ashamed. He couldn't breathe anymore and start coughing. At that moment, Leo found himself lying in his bed in the middle of his tent. A torch lightened the place, and the musty smell of firewood could be perceived from a distance. Yes, he was back in the tent, alone.

"If you know your enemy and know yourself,
You need not fear the result of hundred battles"
- Sun Tzu

He looked around. The table was covered with empty bottles. He reached for a drink and tried to figure out if he had fallen asleep. Then, taking a deep breath, he turned and looked again at the center of the tent. He hesitated if he went to a cave or everything was hallucinations.

"*My shoulder!*" He thought; he quickly rolled his sleeve up. His flesh was intact.

The king touched his head, it was covered with dust, and he felt a little-wet patch with blood. Was this a dream? But, it was so real, and detailed. He was confused, and felt powerless. He did not have time for mysteries and puzzles.

He turned back to the table and struck it with his closed fist. How can a miserable dream mess with his mind now?

He was not a coward, the safety of his kingdom, the honor of his men, and the freedom of his people were a priority. He would ensure the peace in his lands, or fight until the last man.

The images of the cave came to his mind, as well as his defeated army.

"Are we all dying in vain?" A pain in his stomach felt sharp as a knife. *"How can I continue now? Am I losing my mind? Am I going insane?"* He nodded, and remembered the wise voice.

"Doubts, fears, negative thoughts, self-criticism, endless judgments. Those are the real enemies."

He was not to be a prisoner of a private hell. An inferno of evil voices in his head, fears and doubts controlling his will. He was thinking, analyzing too much. He knew faith is not the result of knowledge, but an iron will.

"There's a possibility in every battle!" He thought.

"Hope. Faith, seize of a mustard seed!"–he whispered and knelt to pray. With no strength, he remained on his knees, bowed- the palms of his hands touched the ground. He felt the wind blow in his tent, then in his face. He closed his eyes, an idea lit.

"I AM" – he whispered. He knew what to do now. Color returned to his cheeks. His pulse stabilized. He opened his eyes. The torchlight reflected in his bright pupils.

The young warrior stood up and shouted to his squire- "Andrew! Call my captains. Tonight we are fighting our fears. And we are going to win this war," he said while putting on his armor.

"No coward soul is mine
No trembler in the world's storm-troubled sphere
I see Heaven's glory shine
And Faith shines equal arming me from Fear
Every Existence will exist in thee
There is no room for Death."
- Emily Bronte (fragment)

nine

October, 1523.
Norland Kingdom

"Time is the Fire in Which We Burn"

- Delmore Schwartz

It was 11 o'clock on a Wednesday morning, and Leonard King of Norland had a visible expression of boredom on his pale face. Sitting on an old dark mahogany throne adorned with gold and gems- in a luxurious room. He felt tired already. His mind dwelled in daydreams, and he was constantly yawning.

"It seems that the night didn't grant you any energy, your majesty." Observed Andrew.

"Bloody night! I sleep no more in this cold tomb Andrew. I was awake in the library for hours" –he answered with disdain, finding a comfortable posture in his chair.

Although he looked in his twenties, strong and generally in good health. He never felt good. His sorrow and pains grew; as his affections ended in the cemetery too soon. Everybody aged and died except; he and Andrew.

"Would it be possible to get some of your attention, milord?"

"Uh!" –The King growled. For the young sovereign, life couldn't be more monotonous and dull. One day after another was the same- *"Get up, get dressed, have something to eat, and sit listening to the same complaints over and over. Tedious routine!"* He thought, watching the gleaming light from the windows.

"Every bloody day, waiting for the sun to set to be able to go to my chambers and rest," Leo complained, as audiences were all of the same nature; betrothal problems, debts, and all kinds of legal inquiries. Although the responsibilities were multiple; he reached a point where army's training, production of goods, and the security of the kingdom, became repetitive issues, presenting no challenge.

"Shhh, hash…here they come." Noticed his squire.

"The Duke of Chadwick!" -announced the spokesman with a thud of his staff. Standing next to Leo, Andrew cleared his throat and made a sign to his majesty to compose his posture.

"Your majesty!"-greeted the Duke while bowing.

"Duke," Leo repeated, opening his eyes wide, pretending to be alert. He was dressed in a red and gold doublet. Topped with a fur-lined box coat and lavish chain of office made of gold and encrusted with enormous rubies, typical fashion of European monarchy.

"With great honor, I announce to his majesty that I'm hosting the Zalamandra Count and his honorable family."

"Indeed?"

"His Excellency and party would arrive at Norland in three days, and we are hoping that his Grace grants them his acquaintance," finished the Duke enthusiastically.

"It will be my pleasure to have them as our distinguished guests." He answered, the phrase was almost a perfected practiced line that he had said countless times. He motioned to the castle's chief steward and asked him to prepare a banquet.

"Splendid idea, your majesty," the Duke bowed.

"By all means, Duke." He noticed, pretending interest.

The court murmured. Leo had a bad reputation. The monotony of these events was such that he had launched himself into a life of excesses.

"Silence!" The spokesman hit on the floor once more.

"Yes, Duke. We shall see you and your guests in three nights," said the King, discharging the noble.

"I am very grateful, milord."

"A party?" Whispered Andrew.

Leo's flashed back to the countless times when he had been wasted with alcohol and substances. For decades young women provided him and Andrew with exotic pleasures; Harlots of India, Geishas of Japan, concubines of distant lands, and young ladies from the court. His only motivation was the indulgence of the body.

"Yes, another party" –said with a tedious tone- "I shall be most amused," he whispered while arranging his robe.

"Or unwilling," Andrew noticed. He knew his friend was losing appetite for the sweet permissiveness. Although, for the servant, the practice of hedonism was the only logical way to survive.

Leo's court was divided. Some subjects feared him, and named him "The Immortal King" - but he was not. He only was long-lived. The court felt relief as the Duke, and his "circus" vacated the room. When Leonard looked for his friend, he saw his clumsy servant buried under a mountain of documents; proclamations, edicts, and letters to be answered.

Andrew was unsuccessfully trying to lift a massive stack, and after much effort, he managed to drop it on a table with a loud thud -"these are the issues for today, milord. If we work diligently we shall finish in time for supper."

Leo grimaced in disapproval; he was not to spend another day buried in trivial issues. Life had to offer him more than endless tasks. "No, no…I have had enough for today." He noticed and descended from, the throne ignoring the big stack of papers. He continued talking loudly, speeding his way out of the throne room.

"But, wait…we" -Andrew tried to stop him.

"Instruct the servants to send me something to eat. I need some rest." He almost yelled at his last sentence and made his way to the chamber almost, running leaving his guards behind.

"I'm sick of this predictable life. I shall not live a meaningless life in a golden cage. I choose death instead!" He thought as he climbed the stairs to the tower.

Ten

Immortality

"We only have three minutes to board, Mr. Baylor." Said the Android walking fast through a hall.

Leo hurried after the robot and said in a low voice - "there is a time in life that the future seams eternal, the present unbearable, and life meaningless." He remembered the day he almost finish his existence.

> *"In visions of the dark night*
> *I have dreamed of joy departed*
> *But a waking dream of life and light*
> *Hath left me broken-hearted"*
> *- Edgar Allan Poe*

After leaving the court, King Leonard directed his steps to the highest tower in the castle. He had to stop his madness. If finding the hideous Alchemist to revert the spell was impossible, death had to be the solution. Leonard opened the roof hatch and stood still- as he took one last look at his kingdom. Without hesitation, he jumped off the edge. Seconds in the air, he felt no remorse. His skull fractured upon impact. Blood all over the ground. He felt a sharp ache, then… nothing. He could see his lifeless body on the grown. His spirit was floating around the kingdom; he could see his castle, the woods then a strong emptiness in his heart. He was finally free. His soul was into full light… and a force, an energy that was sucking him violently almost impossible to escape… when...a persistent knock on the door distracted him. The King mumbled something ...“Enter!”

His servant opened the door and came carrying a silver platter with cheese, biscuits and green grapes-“You look awful. Have I interrupted another untimely fantasy of your death?” Andrew mocked him.

“I almost jumped from the tower” Leo ignored him and continued looking at the sky through a narrow window, singing melancholy;

“For the battle, they have forsaken,

For the Glory, they have foretaken,

We tear our worlds apart,

And with this death, I leave you.”

“Oh, I see. You’re ready to be in the box-counting worms?”

“Kyrie Eleison” -Leo ripped the strings of his guitar.

"So, what happened, why you didn't jump from the tower?"

"I resisted the temptation." Leo said arranging his robe and leaving aside his guitar-"Fetch me some tea!"-He said rubbing his eyes, trying to hide his sadness. Andrew rolled his eyes and placed the snacks on a table. He took keys from his pockets and opened a cabinet.

"Andrew, what do you think is the fate of the people who commit suicide?"

"I don't know, Milord; maybe they lose their soul."

"Or maybe they free themselves."

"Well, I have heard stories about it," the servant was looking for a special wine.

"What stories?"

Andrew stopped his search and stared at his master, "people believe that those poor souls remain in Limbo forever, attempting against their lives over and over until they repent."

"Where did you hear that?"

"On the streets, in the taverns....people also talk about how we'll all end paying for our sins in Purgatory. Ah, Eureka!" He showed the wine to this master.

"I don't want to drink. I feel ill."

His friend ignored him, "in today's honor, allow me to indulge you with the essence of fine spirit." The servant filled his glass-"For such a celebration, we'll enjoy an exquisite body and amazing aroma," he tasted the beverage and added pleased, "opulence in a bottle!"

"Celebration, did you say? What's the occasion?" Leo combed his hair with his hands.

"You don't remember?"

"I said, I don't,"

"The battle of Brackenridge, what else?"

"Ah! Indeed,"

"Your people expect a festival before Christmas."

"And they shall have it" - he barged - "as we had enjoyed peace in the realm since the triumph of the army." Leo said excited, "remind me, how many years?"

"Eighty- nine, milord."

"That many…ah,"

'Yes, I can remember clearly that terrible night of …."

"An incredible fight." Interrupted the King proudly –"The camouflage of our soldiers with the dead enemy's uniforms gave us the advantage."

"It was the ditch, your majesty, the ditch we dug at night. That won the battle," remarked Andrew. "Half of the enemy's army perished in it."

Leo raised his glass, "I salute the courage and sacrifice of the warriors who died for King and country,"

"Hail the King," answered the squire and chugged.

"Andrew, how long?" Leo interrupted gloomily.

"Yes."

"How long since Natalie…and my children?" He couldn't finish.

His friend took a moment, then answered, "twelve years, milord." The King was previously married. Seduced by the charms of a noble lady, the sovereign lived a bursting romance. Two healthy boys were the fruit of his intense passion. Unfortunately, his children and wife died victims of a fiber letting him skeptical about life. Memories caught both me.

Leo stood up and approached a window. He stared at the gardens for a few moments -"I detest this loneliness…this overwhelming…."

"Displeasure?"

"Sadness. We're condemned to witness the death of all that surrounds us," he sighed. "Where's the wine?"

"It's gone,"

"Then bring something else, make it strong."

Andrew raised his eyebrows and went back to the wood cabinet.

"Order the preparation of the festival. I would remain in the castle looking at my people from a distance like a shadow."

"Why? We can participate in the festivities."

"No, we can't. They hate me."

"They fear you…it's not the same," the squired added-"But they are not better than you," he offered a drink.

Leo stared at his friend, "I hear the rumors; they say I am an evil man, they believe my longevity is the result of pacts with Satan."

"And is not?"

"Damn you!"

"Ha, you worry too much…don't waste time with rumors. What are these?" Andrew snooped thru papers and parchments. "Oh…I see…maps and charts from the Royal Counsel. What are they looking for?"

"None of your business."

"If you want me to take good care of you…these are my business."

"Thank you nanny! I remind you, I'm your sovereign."

"I won't trouble myself. Your precious secrets are revealed in the corridors of the castle. Every day, as fresh gossip." He smiled and drank from his glass.

"Talking about rumors," Leo approached the table-"This could be the biggest discovery of our time."

"A new world, I heard. A new route to India, or something"

"We don't know yet,"

"Where are your spies?"

"We have spies. Maybe I'll assign you to our next expedition."

"That, I shall enjoy."

Birds were chirping in the garden; golden autumn leaves were falling. Andrew felt satisfied. The friendly chat and the booze worked as planned. But he had to be careful because once his friend started boasting, too much ale would make him high-headed. Andrew re-filled his glass and proposed a game.

"Yesterday, you promised me a revenge," said the servant arranging a chess board for play. "I said. You're becoming a nervous wreck, a wet blanket, Milord."

"Perhaps," Leo wasn't amused with the observation.

"By all means!" Andrew felt the buzz going to his head and said joyfully, "we live, and we die….that's all it is. We please ourselves while it last."

"Mmmm….that simple," reflected the King eating cheese.

"Maybe you need…."

"What do I need?" Asked Leo, sitting next to his friend.

"Female company."

"Lasses!"

"Women, milord…..divine women," he said showing him the queen piece from the chest.

"All are the same sort," Leo said with cynicism- "I'm tired of their game."

"Tired, impossible. Those divine creatures are sensually beautiful…delightfully sinful, and…"

"And fun…I know!" Said the King taking the queen's figure from his friend's hand and placing it on the board.

"You can't deny it; they ease your mind,"

"Or they capture you and take you to the fairies. Proving you're a fool, a complete idiot."

"Simple affair in your case….ha, ha, ha."

"Call me fool once more, I'll send you to the gallows."

"The gallows? I'm your loyal servant, milord."

"You're a loyal pain in my ass." Said Leo looking for his guitar.

Andrew reached for the musical instrument and exclaimed "Ass that I keep clean and safe, I'm afraid."

"Is there such a thing?"

"Indeed." Both men laughed and continued drinking.

Eleven

The Zalamandra Count

A party of several chariots made its way towards the kingdom, down the road. The Zalamandra Count, Don Jose Lorenzo de Gongora led the royal advisors and diplomats that served the purpose of the imperial agenda. The Count was well known and respected as he enjoyed a close relation with his Majesty Fernando II. On that particular night, the Count was on a specific mission, discovering Leo's longevity.

The trip was long and exhausting. Inside an adorned chariot, two young women talked insistently about the Norland sovereign. Their names; Carmen and Lucia Gongora, the lively daughters of the Count.

"How fare are we from the harbor?" Asked Lucia.

"You asked that question minutes ago!" Answered Carmen, the oldest. Bored, Lucia opened a small window of the carriage to look at the forest. The Lorenzo ladies shared an incurable curiosity for Leonard, and their loudmouths didn't stop during the trip.

"Rumors say his kingdom is enchanted too." A cocky smile appeared on their faces.

"Rumors about King Leonard are million, and I'm regretting your presence in this affair. You might be at risk on this trip," answered their father, upset.

"Oh, father, please," complained Lucia.

"You stay away from the wicked man."

"Don't be so severe with the girls, Jose Lorenzo." Ordered his wife.

"That man is evil," answered the father scornfully.

"He's also rich, handsome, and single," noticed Carmen.

"We're not here to find you an unsuitable husband, but to service his majesty, Fernando." Informed Lorenzo and leaned back on a cushion.

"Father, you overwhelm me," complained Carmen. She was a maiden owner of incomparable beauty and a sharp mind. She preferred to be known for her unexpected wit as she was often found in the middle of exiting conversations with some of the intellectuals, scientists, and other smooth talkers. Carmen would get pleasure out of proving a man wrong. Her sister, Lucia, was mostly a sweet and quiet girl that often gave the impression of being dull and irritable.

"You heard me. Stay away from the damn wizard."

"Don't listen to your father," said the Countess.

"We never do!" Answered Lucia, challenging.

Carmen opened her decorated fan and observed, "King Leonard is an eccentric man, that's all."

"He's also a suitable match of an immense fortune, nobility, and repute," said Dona Martina Lorenzo smiling at her husband, who was pretending to be deep in slumber.

"You have it wrong; he has a bad repute," the father answered.

"Bad repute among men, not among ladies," replied Lucia.

"Who, in his right mind, would like to marry an immortal villain?" Asked the Count.

"They say he is complacent with the ladies," Carmen smiled maliciously- "He would not be able to resist me. I'm going to conquer his heart, and grasp his secrets." She sounded confident.

"Maybe, he would share some magic waters from his Fountain of Youth," suggested her mother.

"That would make this dull journey worthy," responded her husband closing his eyes again.

"Carmen, what about the dearly, *Don Ricardo DeSanchez y Montoya*? When did you forget him?" Lucia asked.

Carmen stirred uncomfortably in her seat. Her eyes again fixated on the woods. Dona Martina faced her youngest daughter with disapproval. "How dare you to bring him up?" And she pulled Lucia's dress. "We don't mention his name anymore!"

"That's right, Lucia, Don Ricardo is dead. He died in the wild-land looking for gold." Their father noticed with his eyes closed.

"How insensitive," Martina hit her husband with the fan-"Go back to sleep and hush your mouth!"

"Lucia, I should warn you about something…" Said Carmen with flashy eyes.

"What dear, sis?"

"I won't let King Leonard get-away. I plan to be his crown queen."

"Wow," she clapped to the idea, "and may I ask what your plan is? Maybe you're bringing a secret weapon or potion?"

"You can say that, and it will be irresistible, I assure you." Carmen said and hid a smile behind her open fan.

Twelve

"The adrenaline of playing the game and the satisfaction of winning it; reveals the splendor of life."

"**G**osh!" -cried Andrew as a powerful glow on his face blinded him. He realized he passed out on the king's bed. Next to a chubby body.

"Heavens above, the sun's up!" Noticed a female voice.

"Mildred! What are you doing here, did we sleep together?"

"Oh, no…no…for the love of God. Andrew, you don't remember."

"Remember what?" He was afraid of the answer.

"I brought you food, milord. You woke me up in the middle of the night. His majesty was hungry."

"Oh, yes, yes…I remember."

"We ate and drink. The King played his guitar and hee hee hee" –the cook had her cheeks pink, and her breath reeked of alcohol.

"What is so funny?

"Nothing…nothing, milord!" She couldn't talk about her king's foulness-"I have to go now," the middle age cook ran out of the room.

"You better mention this incident to no one."

"I was never in this room," the woman said, exiting fast. She slapped the door behind her. The loud noise woke up Leo.

"Andrew, I cannot move," he was face down at the foot of his bed, semi-naked and with his shoes still on. He was holding his guitar.

"Allow me, milord."

"Oh, my back," said Leo, holding his temples.

"Easy!"

"Ogg…my head!"

Andrew dropped his master on the bed and ran to the table.

"Bless my soul. I'm hungry as a bear," the servant said, reaching some trays -"Want a bite?"

"I want nothing. Just disappear from my sight." Exclaimed Leo, but Andrew ignored his friend and took a piece of ham and a spoon filled with baked apples, then drank from a pitcher.

"Is that water?" Leo asked by seeing how the liquid dripped down his friend's chin. The servant nodded his head, and Leo jumped out and grabbed the pitcher to drink, then took a lemon and squeezed it in his mouth to finally disappear into the sheets, covering his swollen face-"Close the door, gently. I can't stand any damn noise."

"You should eat."

"LEAVE ME ALONE!"

"Irony of life -the poor man seeks for food, the rich for appetite," said the servant, eating merrily. "Milord, sink into a soft bed, is not helping your cause."

"What cause?" Leo asked under the sheets.

"We should ride all day... to the North," Andrew said, chewing.

"Rubbish."

"Head to the woods. Fill our lungs... with fresh air."

"NO!"

"You've been overwhelmed with responsibilities, and a big agenda." Andrew wanted to prevent his friend from more self-pity. Leo's confessions of last night worried the squire. The young monarch was taking the morbid suicidal fantasies too seriously.

"Andrew, get out, pull the curtains... and tip-toe to the door."

"If you sleep now," he paused, savoring every bite, "You'll be... up all night... and the pending issues would double,"- he said with heavy wit. The King jumped from the bed and cried- "How many pending audiences we have?" he approached a mirror, but he didn't like what he saw.

"A lot."

"I look like bloody shit."

"You look worse than bloody shit."

"It feels like the whole world is looking for something. What do they expect from me?"

"Your subjects need your approval, milord. They're looking for comfort for their souls and bellies."

"And where is my comfort, I ask?" said Leo touching his head staring at a mirror. "Is today Wednesday?" He splashed water on his face.

"Thursday."

He sank his face in a towel wishing to heal his spirit, "I need to recover, before I return to face them. They can't see me like this."

"A wise monarch you are, Sir." Andrew smiled, offering a clean suit to his master. "Nothing like filling the lungs with fresh air. Nature cures the heart, and easy the minds."

"Don't trick me, Andrew. I'm not your buffoon. I know you well."

"So, you must agree that we share this evil curse of immortality, and we're in the affliction together."

Gouf

On that cold morning, the two men rode with an escort of soldiers to the north of the kingdom. It was always fun to see the vast emerald green meadows, full of cattle and sheep, resembling a perfect canvas. Nevertheless, the scented forest was an all-time favorite. Fall was present in every corner as they penetrated the heart of the habitat. The fantastic colored range of leaves was changing from green to orange reaching almost copper tones. The northern forest was a magical place filled with wandering spirits who whisper gently to the visitor's hearts.

"Brilliant idea, Andrew. The forest is my favorite," the King said, crossing a row of elms and cedars. The fresh aroma of the woods calmed the visitor's senses. Home of fairies, goblins, and gnomes; all invisible to the human eye, yet perceptible by crossing an abundant pad of evergreen and oaks.

"And into the forest, I go, to lose my mind and find my soul," sang Andrew. The west wind brought a perfumed breeze, making the leaves of the trees touch each other as if they were singing. Leo was a passionate nature lover; he stopped next to one oak with a robust trunk and leafy branches.

"Magnificent tree!" Leo noticed- "Tall and strong. Probably a hundred years old," he touched the trunk and observed- "Fulfil its destiny without suffering. It simply flowers."

"It does…. for hundreds of years. Time adds layers to the truck, making it stronger," observed Andrew.

Leo cracked a smile; he eased his mind. His spirit felt free, like the chipping birds in the trees. The men continued their day trip in complete silence, enjoying the natural music of the forest. The soft breeze refreshed the air with a salty aroma when they arrived next to the ocean. In the distance, it was possible to detect a small group of men talking to some shepherds.

"Are those our knights?" Asked the King to his companions.

"Sure they are."

When the men saw the King, they stopped and turned to greet him.

"Your majesty, excellent day for a ride!" Sir Maurice greeted.

"What am I interrupting?" Leo asked, dismounting his horse.

"We are playing gouf,"

"What type of a game is this?" Leo asked, taking off his globes.

"Allow us to show you while we play," replied one man.

The soldiers play on green grass as immaculate as a turquoise carpet. They were amused by the task of putting little balls inside some quirky rabbit holes.

"Interesting." Leo observed, "I want to try."

"By all means!" Maurice, the oldest warrior, bowed.

"Skip the protocol. Instruct me."

"You see, milord, the objective," Maurice explained, "is to strike the ball as hard as possible. The target is the round green in the distance. The one with the small basket whipping in the wind."

The men soaked in the vastness of the rolling fields before them, like a green canvas just waiting for an artist's brush. One of the knights held a small ball and placed it atop a little mound of dirt. Standing next to it, he took a slow practice swing with a wooden stick he had pulled from a large bag. Leo smiled with serious interest. Squinting to see the little basket. Soon he was playing too.

"Do not allow your ball to go into a bunker, milord." Stated one of the knights. Pointing to a depression of what looked like dirt and sand.

"On the green is a four-inch hole, and we roll the ball into the hole in the fewest strokes possible," stated Maurice.

Leo, now ready to begin the round, stood frozen for what seemed an eternity, before swinging the club back and around his broad shoulders. He hit the ball with tremendous speed, and the air cracked like thunder -as the club met the ball. In an instant, it soared through the blue sky as if pinned against the very clouds themselves.

Time seemed to stand-still. Then, the ball landed with a thud, almost in the center of the fairway, and the King clapped in approval.

"Excellent! Now," explained Maurice, "let's walk to the ball and hit it again, this time trying to land it on the green." To everyone's surprise, Leonard grabbed the bag of clubs and tossed it over his shoulder, but Andrew immediately caught up to him and asked- "allow me, your majesty."

"Certainly, certainly Andrew," he tapped his back.

The young squire noticed the urgency and excitement in his master's eyes with satisfaction. Leo stood next to the ball and pondered just how to advance it towards the target. The breeze had picked up and was now against the men, as they surveyed the course.

Leo selected a club randomly and stood next to the ball, took a mighty swing, and then watched with excitement to see it land. He looked around like a child searching for his favorite toy.

"Extraordinary!" Shouted Maurice, "Milord, you are on the green!"

His majesty roared with delight as an air of passionate thrill came over the men.

"Now what?"

The hole is small. This driving club is too large. Maurice selected a thinner club reaching into the bag, and handed it to Leo.

"Here," Maurice said excitedly, "this is a putter, and it's made to roll the ball to the hole."

One of the knights demonstrated a putting stroke. Cautiously, Leo rolled the ball, which disappeared into the hole with a pleasant clinking sound. He jumped into the air and shouted.

"Let's do it again!" The sovereign understood the nature of the game immediately. The contest was within. Dominating the game had to be his new obsession. Andrew was smiling, watching his friend play for hours, finally able to ease his mind.

"*Mighty game, he's being completely distracted.*" Thought his friend with satisfaction, while the flight of seagulls and the sound of the waves crashing on the sea composed a perfect postcard. The men played with enthusiasm until the last rays of sunlight. Leonard stopped and told his warriors- "This game excited me. It's invigorating. I have not been so delighted in years." He took a deep breath and added- "only one thing bothered me."

Everybody stared at him.

"I don't like the name, gouf. I'll change it to golf, and we shall play it in the realm."

The warriors cheered their leader. The game became a national gem and offered them great joy and entertainment. An incomparable sense of achievement would shape their characters like nothing else in this world.

> *"The game was invented a billion years ago-*
> *Don't you remember?"*
> *-old Scottish saying*

Back in the castle, everybody was busy preparing for the visit. The kitchen was full of servants involved in hard work. Large iron caldrons were bubbling with soups and stews on the fires. Comfort food that harbored the soul with warm ingredients. On the floor, baskets and sacks containing vegetables were all over the place. The tables were full of condiments; buckets with fresh milk, honey, cheese, spices, and herbs. Lambs, cattle, chicken, and fowl were tethered or in cages near the kitchen. A pond stocked with fish and cooking herbs was grown in the gardens.

The group of soldiers and gentlemen rode back to the castle in very good spirits. Leo's cheeks were pink, and his hair was slightly amiss when he ran directly to the kitchen with incredible energy. As soon as Leo entered the room, everybody froze in disbelief. In years, a royal member had never set foot in the back of the castle. Unaware of his presence, the King kept strutting through the room with confidence, eyeing all the goodies on the tables, as if deciding what to indulge in first.

"Owen!" Called Leo.

"Yes, your majesty," answered the steward.

"There's a party of gentlemen in the hall waiting to be served…what's that smell?" A large loaf of fresh bread was out of the oven on the table. He walked closer and cut a slice, added some butter, and stuffed it in his mouth with carelessness. Andrew was busy tasting the stews from the cauldrons and grabbing a young lady from behind. "Outch, Andrew, you moron!"-Said the girl upset pushing him away, while Leonard was busy talking to a cook- "I want… for supper…stew and…" the aroma of baked chicken hit Leo's face, "Oh! That looks magnificent, Mildred."

"It's ready, milord," the chubby cook took out of the oven a crispy caramelized bird cooked with herbs.

"Owen, my good friend," the King touched the servant's shoulder, "I was ill and unwell for weeks, but today the good Lord granted me back my appetite."

"Bless be the Lord, milord." Said the steward with reverence.

Leo said joyfully, "all of you… do a superb job." The service was confused for a second; then, they smiled back at him, feeling pride.

"And you Owen… you too, Mildred. Everybody, should be ready for our guests. The Count of Zalamadra would arrive tomorrow," he announced while exiting the kitchen quickly- "Now serve us supper!"

"Yes, milord," answered Owen, feeling flattered and awed by the unexpected change in his master's mood.

Thirteen

The Game we play

It was Friday and close to noon when an exuberant banquet to the taste of his royal highness was ready. Servants and cooks were finalizing details decorating the Great Hall with flowers and golden plates that gleaned by the light of candles.

"We're almost ready, Milord," announced the steward of the castle. Leo felt refreshed as he was finally getting enough sleep, "everything looks splendid. Thank you, Owen." He remarked, satisfied.

"The entertainment is new, Milord and of high quality; exhibitions with knights and tournaments."

"Good…"

"Jugglers, musicians, and acrobats are scheduled for a day of enjoyment of your special guest," informed the servant with a pompous attitude, "we'll start with refreshments and a dance."

"Excellent," Leonard said, walking fast through the room with scrutiny eyes. The fanfares trumpets sounded. The invitees arrived; diplomats, guests of honor, and then three women. The head steward announced them: Count Don Jose Maria Lorenzo, his wife, Countess Dona Martina, and her two daughters, Carmen and Lucia. Rousing curiosity seized the court. Everybody froze by admiring the costumes of the ladies. They were exceptional and innovative.

Carmen, Lucia, and Dona Maria looked like living dolls, wearing the latest fashions; long cinched gowns, with embroidered back work. Their long skirts were accentuated by their voluminous Spanish farthingales. A new exciting fashion from the South, compared to the bored high-waist dresses of Norland.

Don Felipe Salazar y Hurtado, Ambassador to the Spanish King, captured many eyes with his sparkling personality. He stepped in front of the ladies and bowel to the King, and his court exclaiming as loud as he could –"It's a great honor to be guests of such a distinguished Kingdom."

Leo was standing in the main room eagerly. Ready to welcome them. He met the Ambassador and returned the compliment- "The pleasure is mine. Please gentlemen, refresh yourself after your long journey." He said staring at Carmen, the young maiden- dressed in red. The King felt a chill all over his body when he offered his arm to the lady. Her incredible brown eyes were bright like gems. Her brown hair resembled pure silk. Her body was of a statuesque perfection; a voluptuous diva was Carmen, who looked at him flirtatious. Next, the living goddess smiled at him, with thick ruby lips ready to explore his body. She was an eager invitation to a passionate affair. The fantastic creature slapped the eyes of the King, leaving him breathless. Leonard conducted the party to his table and made a sign for them to sit and enjoy the banquet. Then, he welcomed them with a brief speech.

"I'm delighted with the visit of the Count of Zalamandra and his honorable family to the kingdom of Norland. It's with great pleasure that I welcome the honorable guests. Let the festivity commence." He said and made a sign for the servants to start the banquet.

Leo constantly looked at Carmen. She hardly ate, and his majesty decided he had to be closer to the lady. When the dance began. Carmen was sensual and flirtatious while dancing, and she managed to be next to Leo the rest for the party. She was easy-going. Laughing and complementing the young sovereign. Ambassador Felipe looked uncomfortable and stared at them, full of jealousy. Soon, everybody was outside the castle, witnessing knight's tournaments.

Leonard was aware of the Ambassadors presence and deliberately flirted with the lady. Before finishing the last tournament, the sun went down, and cold winds blew outside the castle.

Carmen approached Leo and surprised him with a request – "It's too cold for me, milord. Would it be possible that you take me near a fire inside?" She asked in an inviting tone.

"By all means, milady." He grabbed her hand and kissed her knuckles while glancing up into her eyes. The lady looked at him, giving him a blast of sexual heat. He made a sign for the next tournament to start, then took her by the arm and walked to the castle. He intended to be alone with the lady, so they rapidly entered the library. He was aware of a presence behind him. Someone followed them, and he hastened to close the door.

"Amazing room." Carmen glanced.

"Not as amazing as you," he remarked. The room, full of books, was distinguished for its giant fireplace, which painted the library with coral lights. "Thank you for allowing me into a library." She got closed to the fireplace.

"In my kingdom, there is no prohibition for the ladies to read and consult books."

"Ah, how uncommon!"

"I know, I'm pretty uncommon. I've an odd reputation. Visitors are not frequent in this land."

She smiled at him.

"Your kingdom is singular….your reputation, exceptional I must say."

"Do you fear me?"

"Should I?"

Leonard was amused, "allow me to offer you a beverage to warm you."

"Thank you,"

The library had two levels, and books from distant lands covered the room wall to wall. Leonard felt pride in displaying his collection.

"I guess you spend a good amount of time in this room," she said with her cute accent, as she took a book with a leather cover.

"Desde luego," he answered in Spanish and offered her a glass- "This is my hiding place. I spend hours in this room surrounded by innovative ideas." He stared at her beautiful eyes covered with thick eyelashes. "I'm proud of my collection," Leo noticed an enormous ruby ring adorning one of her soft hands.

"What type of books does his majesty own?"

"All types, old, new, some are in dialects… even Greek!"

"Do you mean?" She lowered her voice, "prohibited books?" Her eyes sparkled. Leo cracked a smile and repeated, *"Profana text!"*- Carmen giggled.

The king proposed a toast, "for this pleasant encounter."

"For us!" She answered, drinking all the content of her glass.

She closed her eyes and exclaimed satisfied -"Ah, just what I needed." Leo smiled pleased, her expression turned him on. Carmen reached into her pocket and offered him a beautiful carved wooden box, "I took the liberty of bringing you a present, your majesty" -Sensuality was around her. Leo was enchanted with the charming maiden. He was ready to roll the dice and play her game.

"More gifts, I'm excited," he noticed, effusively. He was already presented with a serial of crafts from Zalamandra.

"This one is special. You see… this one is personal."

"Thanks," Leo opened the carved box. "Nice box… A spyglass," he exclaimed, taking the small telescope out of the box. Noticing it was of exceptional quality. The lady moved closer to him. If Leo could read her mind, he would be listening to an open invitation to love her.

"You have to remember your majesty; sometimes the containers are more valuable than the essences," by saying this, Carmen opened her full lips, uncommonly sensual, as a sign for an inviting kiss.

Leo tried to kiss her, but she covered her face with her fan and giggled, which Leo removed immediately and kissed her impetuously. His body was stroked by passion. The chemistry among both bodies was pure fire.

All blushed; Leonard, cleared his throat and excused himself, aware of the danger of the temptation- "Pardon me milady, I am being imprudent."

"Not at all!" She saw the iris in his eyes getting bigger as she got closer, "be imprudent…" -she touched his chest with her excited nipples. The exquisite sensation excited the young man, who gently pulled the lady closer, squishing her cheeks, and kissed her with a passion that seemed to last an eternity- "Take me to your private chamber," she whispered in his ear, as she was caressing his neck with her lips. The seduction game was on. He pushed the wall behind him, a connecting passageway that led to his private chamber. In his room, he started to undress her; the beauty of her body was breathtaking. Full and rounded hips appeared under her robes. He approached her and began touring them with his big hands, touching her thighs. Carmen loved every touch from Leo and responded with passionate kisses all over his muscular body, which was stripped naked in seconds. Burning as a torch, he removed the rest of her clothes to reveal rounded, perfect breasts. Gently, they fell to the bed as Leo fumbled with the rest of her gown- Carmen found ecstasy in Leonard's body. She was a perfect receptor for his sexual energy; her moans of pleasure made him transcend to a level of high awareness. Every inch of her was pure fire; every touch, every caress, gave life to the young man. The possession of that woman made the King fall into a delightful state of mind. Exhausted, they collapsed into each other's arms. Soon, both lovers were quiet, peaceful silence reigned in the room. The young King kissed her forehead gratefully, he felt joy. Leo slept for hours, letting his mind to be full of expectations for the future with the young maiden.

Fourteen

Dried Blood

The Duke of Chadwick rose early before dawn. It was a ritual that he believed brought him peace and prosperity. After the last corner of the sky was drowning in sunlight, James Chadwick closed his eyes and took a couple of deep breaths clearing his mind completely. He was satisfied with the reaction of the King to the lady from Zalamandra. Full of pride in his matchmaker, he allowed himself to daydream about a commitment between the couple. An alliance signed between both kingdoms with a royal wedding, securing the Duke's immense fortune. He was sure that the massive movement of ships and troops from the King of Spain was due to discovering new lands, and great treasures. The Duke entered the castle optimistically after saying his prays, when he heard a piercing scream. James Chadwick ran as fast as his legs allowed him to see people hysterically running all over the place.

"HELP....HELP! -They were shouting.

Carmen

On the other side of the castle, Leo woke up a different man. He noticed that the lady was no longer sleeping by his side, to his dismay. He was about to go and look for her, when Andrew opened the curtains.

"Wow, easy with the light!"

"It's a beautiful morning, and I brought you breakfast."

"What is the emergency? It has to be close to dawn."

"We have guests," Andy answered, pretending not to know about the affair. However, the entire court was gossiping about it.

"I'm starving. I can eat an ox. Let's see what you have...?" Asked Leo, and reached for a tray. The young monarch could feel his bed full of Carmen's distinctive aroma of orange leaves and flowers.

"Where is Carmen?" He asked while chewing a bite.

"Who?"

"Our lovely guest from Zalamandra! We had an encounter last night," he added- "I guess you know..."

"Ha, sure I know. I did notice the spark in your eyes."

"You did? …Interesting," Leo felt his spirit rise again, "I cannot wait to have that beauty in my arms," he whispered and felt relieved the young lady was discreet enough to move to her chamber, but Andrew didn't answer. He was walking towards the door.

"What is that noise? Someone is shouting," the squire opened the door.

"Get, Help! Somebody… "

"What is that commotion?" Leo jumped out of his bed. Owen stormed in, followed by an army of servants and soldiers. "There is an urgency for your presence, Milord! Said the butler pail.

"What is it?"

"It's a tragedy, milord. In the west wing," he answered, trying to control his shaking hands.

The men rushed towards the main hall. Andrew asked a member of the guard to follow them. They ran up the tower skipping two steps at a time. Once they arrived, they looked perplexed at the scene. They walked inside Carmen's chamber; the door was ajar. Lucia was sitting by the bed, sobbing. Carmen's body was hanging from the neck of a chandelier. She was pale and lifeless; the gorgeous creature was white as a piece of paper with eyes closed. Leo immediately felt dizzy, the Duke nauseous. Dark death covered the room completely.

"Help me, gentlemen," asked Leonard, who approached her carefully and unhooked the body with the help of Owen and

Andrew. They placed her corpse on the bed. Leo touched her face, now cold as ice. Then he took her hands into his. "Milady," he whispered with reverence and kissed her hands. Carmen was still beautiful. Her expression was melancholic. He noticed the ruby ring was not on her finger anymore.

"Is she…?" Asked her sister, covering her mouth.

"Yes, she's dead." Answered Leo, gloomily.

Suddenly, a hysterical Lucia crawled to the foot of the bed and cried. "Noooo, HAY DIOS MIO….DIOS MIO!"

At the entrance of the chamber were Carmen's parents. They were looking with pale expressions, hoping all was a charade. In an instant, the mother of the victim fainted.

"Take your wife to her room." Said Leo to the Count, "Andrew, be sure they get whatever they need."

"Yes, your majesty."

Leo excused himself and ordered Owen to follow him into a private room. Alone and with the door locked, Leo inquired- "What happened, Owen?"

"Milord, this morning, we were preparing breakfast for your guests; it was still dark. Andrew came for a tray for you. When the sun came up, I heard the screams of a woman," the servant was pale and took a deep breath- "she was screaming pronto…pronto…help me, my sister. I ran to her as fast as I could, then I saw the body of the lady hanging from the ceiling. She killed herself, milord!"

"That woman has been dead for several hours," remarked Leo.

"Her body is cold as ice." Noticed the servant, frightened. They were interrupted by a knock on the door; Owen opened the golden doorknob, allowing the Duke of Chadwick into the room.

"The lady did not kill herself; this is not suicide," affirmed the old man full of anger.

"I bet my soul, Duke." Leo agreed. He knew Carmen was delighted with him last night. She had no reason to kill herself. "What do you know?"-Asked Leo, sitting on a chair offering one to his friend.

"I just examined the body. Only to verify there was nothing else out of the ordinary."

"AND?"

"I found a wound on her skull," he nodded- "Dried blood on her hair. She died of a blow to the head." His words struck alarm in the room.

"Are you saying……that she was murdered?"

"So it seems, your majesty. Nothing but calculated shambles."

"God will have mercy of her soul." The King exclaimed and looked perplexed to the men.

Fifteen

The castle got into a commotion; people were busy coming and going while Carmen's mother remained unconscious despite given salts to wake up.

Finally, the King dispatched everyone to their houses, guests and others planned as entertainment for the visit. On a very dark night, the service arranged everything for the young lady's funeral. A coffin was provided and after fixing the body, everybody in the castle attended the visitation in the chapel.

Leo apologized, and went to his hidden spot, at approximately two in the morning. He was disappointed; his mind was puzzled, his spirit uneasy. Half passed out after some guilt-ridden drinking. He had imprinted the lady's memory, and recalled her with each sip to a bottle of whiskey.

"Burning flame of my heart's desire was…Carmen!" The notes from his guitar were a posthumous homage.

"I've tried to kill myself so many times. Now I know that would never happen, but you Carmen, sensual angel. You end in a cold grave with mortal damage."

At this time, Leonard was sure she didn't commit suicide. He wanted to prove Carmen was a victim of murder, he couldn't think clearly, an insisting knocking on the door distracted him. He knew it had to be Andrew.

"Leave me alone!" -He cried and took the bottle in his mouth to the last drop. Anger conquered his mind. He wanted to revenge the murder. Find the evil that cut short Carmen's blossoming life. In his mind, there was nothing but a keen impulse to avenge her death. He could not fathom why anyone harmed such a graceful creature.

"Sweet creatures are the lasses, vulnerable and tender. I hate to see them hurt." He said to *Richard,* his cat, who jumped on his lap and interrupted his meditation. His little friend crawled on his legs and meowed as Leo caressed him. "Yes, friend, we are involve in a scandal. Imagine the gossiping's around us. The condemnation and judgment to the immortal wizard king of Norland" –He said, heartbroken. His grey kitty jumped on a table next to Carmen's present, like trying to call his master's attention. Leo stood up and opened the box, then took the spyglass in his hands.

"Why…why she was murdered?" Maybe she knew a secret. What could it be? He opened the spyglass and found a piece of paper inside in Latin:

"Sol non est occultatum in terra. The sun doesn't set on my lands" – He repeated and remembered the moment she gave him the present.

"You have to remember your majesty, sometimes, the containers are more valuable than the essences." Those were her words; then he focused on the carved box - it was carved with figures embossed. There was the sun, three stars, and a symbol.

"The symbol of gold!" He realized-"The three stars with an inclination to the left" He touched the stars.

"Tree stars…three alleged ships." – Interesting, he realized.

"Sol non est ocultatum in terra…he repeated once more. If the sun doesn't set on land…therefore it moves!"- Leo murmured, and he turned the sun to the right in a clockwise movement. Next, he pushed down the three stars by instint, starting with the one closest to the sun to the west.

"Let's see…if this works," he said. Finally, he pushed the symbol of gold. The box clicked, and a secret compartment opened. A slit was barely visible. "Eureka!"- He felt the edge of the box with his fingers. He raised the box to the level of his eyes. He couldn't find a good reason for such abstruseness, and indeed, he didn't believe in coincidences. He peeked into the narrow slit, and sure enough, a folded piece of paper was carefully lodged in it.

"A map….of course, it's a map!" He exclaimed and unfolded the parchment. It was a chart showing land across the Atlantic, and a treasure city called Tenoxtitlan. Leonard was breathless. Carmen knew about the treasure and the discovery of the land.

"Click!" Someone inserted a key in the lock; the door opened, Andy came inside with a candle in his hand.

"Milord" He called him softly.

"What is it?"-Leo hid the map in his lap.

"The Duke needs to talk to you."

"Let me alone, RESPECT MY GRIEF!"

The servant was pail and decided to inform his friend directly. "Your bedchamber maid found this candlestick next to your bed, this morning while cleaning…"

"What's so odd? …You looked disturbed."

"It has blood, milord. Dried blood, and human hair." He answered in a worried voice. "The hair matches the deceased."

"Do you think I hit her?"

"Not me, Leonard…her father is suggesting…"

"What? …What is he suggesting?"

"He's asking for an audience."

Leo couldn't believe his ears. He felt anger as burning fire and cried "I'm stopping this bloody game!" He vigorously rose from his chair allowing the box on his lap to drop loudly to the floor.

Ruby Ring

The Duke and guest were sitting down in the tea room. The place was lit by chandeliers, and the light of a crescent moon shone through an open window. Dawn was expected soon, and the women hadn't stopped sobbing. They had to be literally dragged across the manor, so they could have something to drink and eat. The Zalamadra Count looked somber and distant, obviously hurt by the death of his daughter.

"A message has being sent to his majesty, Fernando II," said the Ambassador approaching the victim's father. "An investigation will be conducted, and the one responsible for this atrocity will be found."

"You've spoken with righteous judgment, Ambassador," said Leo entering the room. "That is exactly what I intend to do." And he looked at Felipe sharply.

The Ambassador approached the King and said coldly, "if you don't provide justice to this family, the King of Spain will revenge this offense!"

"There will be no more arguments," said Leo- "I'll expose the perpetrator of this crime," he got close to Felipe and added, "the responsible won't leave my castle alive…" he touched the young man's chest, and growled- "And you can inform this to your King!"

The ladies broke into tears. That was the opportunity the Duke of Chadwick was waiting for. He took advantage of the commotion and discreetly went to the top of the tower searching for evidence. He arrived in Carmen's room, swung the door open, and lit the room with a candle; it was mainly undisturbed. Chills went down his spine. He tried to look around for signs of violence. He looked at all the décor. Neatly placed upon the furniture, the portraits hanging from the stone walls were all straight, and dusty. They had not been moved. He looked around to see if the tapestries had been disturbed, nothing, the room was clean. He closed the door slowly, careful not to make any noise. Then he crossed the hallway and went to Lucia's room. The sick child had cried all day.

The Duke was happy she was not around. Then he noticed it, a small dark stain on the floor. He got down on one knee and held the candle closer to the rug. He scratched it with his fingernail. "*Blood!*"

He shone the flame further away from the door and noticed another small stain not far from the first one. He kept on looking. Then found the third one. This was a trail.

"Definitely, put some facts into perspective," the Duke said to himself when he noticed a red glow next to the leg of the bed. It was a ruby ring glowing in the dark. He placed the ring into his pocket and left the room. He ran to the stairs looking for Leonard.

> *"With immense rage, I killed you.*
> *By becoming your executor,*
> *I mortally wound myself."*

"Yes, I recognize the ring," said Leo examining the jewel-"She wore it the night we met. Yet, this doesn't prove anything, Duke."

"It proves that Carmen was killed in Lucia's room."

"Possibly, but you don't think her sister did it?"

"I don't know what to believe, but if you allow me. I can interview the servants in the castle. I'm sure someone saw or heard something to solve the mystery."

"Excellent idea," exclaimed Leo.

A line of servants came with information. One by one interviewed by the Duke. Leo's maid saw Ambassador Felipe exiting the King's bedchamber on the morning of the murder. Ana, the maid in charge of cleaning and maintaining fireplaces, heard two women arguing in a foreign language the night they arrived.

"Did you enter their room?" -asked the Duke.

"No, because I saw the ladies arguing."

"Did you understand the words they spoke?"

"No, milord….but I saw the deceased lady slap the face of her young sister. It was when I left the floor."

Mildred, the cook was ready to go to her room after locking the pantry. When she took the stairs, she saw the shadow of a man carrying a woman into the victim's chamber. She said, she dismissed it, assuming a guest had too much ale. The Duke, the King, and other advisors remained all night in the library. The investigation was almost complete. They were exhausted, and the sun was shining on a new day.

"Gentlemen, we've collected good information. The resolution we have arrived at has to be correct. Now, go to your chambers and rest some,"- said the King when Andrew abruptly opened the heavy door.

"Your majesty, we have another problem," said his friend alarmed.

"Speak!"

"Ambassador Felipe."

"Yes?"

"Was found dead, in his chamber."

"Poisoned, I presume."

"Yes, milord… with arsenic."

"As we expected," said Leonard to his advisors.

 Sixteen

Trial

It was Wednesday afternoon, and chariots were still arriving at the castle. The main hall was crowded. Lady Martina asked for a chair. She was continually smelling salts to prevent her from fainting again. The unexpected death of her oldest daughter made her very ill.

"How long must we deal with this situation?" Asked the Count, desperately to his assistant. The Duke heard him and felt sympathetic with his guest. Chadwick made efforts to comfort him.

"We all share the same concern Count, and we expect the resolution of this situation," said the Duke, who was looking for the steward of the castle to ask how long they had to wait for the King, while several members of Parliament were taking places at the court to perform as a jury.

Finally, Leonard appeared in a flash, holding papers in his hands.

"My deepest apologies to all of you for the delay," he said and sat on the throne. He cleared his throat and continued- "I'm calling the Parliament to hold a trial on the murders of Carmen de Lorenzo and Ambassador Felipe Sanchez." A loud murmur was produced in the room. Leo continued- "This court will prove that Lady Carmen de Lorenzo was beaten with a candlestick, then choked to death, and hung from a chandelier. All this to disguise her death as a suicide."

"Oooh," the crowd was shocked.

The King continued- "We also know that Ambassador Don Felipe Sanchez y Hurtado was silenced with arsenic."

"Ah!" Carmen's mother was crying loudly.

"An investigation was conducted regarding both crimes by the Duke of Chadwick, advisors, members of my personal guard, and myself."

Leo addressed his audience- "In my realm, the practice of torture of prisoners to confess their crimes had been reduced to the minimum. So, we collected several pieces of evidence that will be presented to you to proceed with the trial." Leonard made a sign, and two guards stood behind Lucia Lorenzo.

"What is the meaning of this?" Lucia's father inquired.

Leonard explained- "On the day of the ball, this map of a golden treasure was handed to me by Carmen, your daughter. I strongly believe that the lady had the intention of becoming my wife, and she was offering this information to me as part of our common fortune."

The noise in the room went louder. The King raised his voice.

"Lady Carmen was the owner of great beauty, and she was rewarded for her charms. Charms that had a tremendous impact on me." Finished Leonard.

"So, you killed her!" Carmen's father shouted.

"On the contrary, I loved her."

"You shameless and cynical man, you are not a gentleman, but the face of pure evil!"

"Silence." The steward ordered.

Leo ignore Carmen's father, but he was aware of the impact of those words in the court, he raised his voice and said- "the map was not the only document she handled me."

The jury's eyes were looking at him attentively as he showed another document.

"This is a written confession signed by Carmen accusing Don Felipe and her sister Lucia of a conspiracy and an attempt to murder her" -he added- "Carmen stated in this document that her sister and Don Felipe knew of the existence of the map, apparently the property of the King of Spain, and they were looking for it."

"Arrest Lucia de Lorenzo!" Shouted the Duke.

"NO!" -cried her father, pulling out his sword attacking the guards.

At the sign of his majesty, more guards struggled with him and took him, prisoner. Lucia ran towards the King, trying to snatch the note written by her sister. Leo stopped her and asked- "Why you were arguing with Carmen the night of her death? Were you looking for the map?"

"Yes, I asked her for the map"- she confessed –"Carmen denied having it, and she threatened me by saying she would be the queen of Norland."

"Then you hit her with the stick,"

"It was an accident...I was mad…She said Felipe was using me. She lied."

"How did she lie?"

"She insulted me, she said Felipe was in love with her!" -Her face was red with fury.

"She didn't lie. Felipe was in love with her," clarified the Duke, standing next to the King- "That was obvious…young lady."

"But I loved Felipe; he was already my lover," cried Lucia with eyes of fire.

"Felipe hung Carmen from the ceiling, because you wounded her mortally with the candle-stick," said Leonard bitterly.

"She was already dead, I killed my sister by an accident. Felipe and I wanted to blame you!"

"Why did you poison him last night?" -asked the Duke.

"He was going to betray me."

"Felipe was ready to testify against you," stated the Duke.

"Unless I provided him with the map, but I couldn't find it."

"No, because the map is in my possession, and you didn't know…poor child." Said Leo.

"Oh, my God…no...no..." -she cried, covering her face, "I was so jealous," then, she attacked the King physically. "It's all your fault….you damn wizard," the guards stop her.

Next, she spoke in Spanish- "Mama, perdon" and ran to her mother's arms. Dona Martina de Lorenzo was not sure of what happened. She hugged her daughter, but the guards took Lucia prisoner. Martina asked to her husband- "Que esta pasando? Sagrado Corazon...They can't take my baby!" She became frenetically.

Leonard rose from his throne, and with a loud voice announced.

"I have to apprehend Lucia Lorenzo present in this room, charged with the murder of Lady Carmen and Ambassador Felipe" - and added- "I am taking you as the witness of her confession. A sentence would be dictated to the prisoner in brief," the jury agreed.

Leo walked a few steps and addressed the parents of the young ladies, touching his heart, he said- "My deepest condolences, your graces," and he gave them back the map. "Please deliver this to his majesty and prepare for your return."

"Ah," Dona Lucia cried with horror by listening to his words and hid her face on her husband's chest.

Seventeen

Sentence

Leonard heard his servant coming to the chamber.

"I can't believe…" -Andy said and left the door open- "There's the biggest commotion out there."

"I know, I'm busy Andrew, I've work to do," mumbled Leo with disdain-"That habit of yours…interrupting me…. " He said while finishing writing.

"So, there is a treasure and a new world…rumors are true."

"Yes." Leo got up from his chair with a face agitated by anger – "I'm having problems with Lucia's Sentence," he said, soaking a long feather into an ink bottle-"Maybe you can help."

"Me?"

"Yes, you. I'm exhausted"- He sat again, signed and sealed the edicts using red candle wax and royal stamp.

"But, milord we cannot waste time; the kingdom of the South is rich in gold and treasures."

"Not only that," he rolled a parchment- "The Spanish King would consolidate several colonies into one empire." Said Leo, stretching his arms over his head.

"We should send expeditions to the new world. Claim our piece!"

"We will."

Andrew was agitated and inquiring, "but you returned the map."

"The scribes made a copy of it. You see, we do have spies." He walked to the door, "I need some rest; I'm exhausted."

"Wait! How did you know Lucia was the offender?"

"Just a week ago, I was telling you about this awful emptiness I feel, this crushing depression that takes my appetite and sleep. My desire for life."

"Yes…yes…but how did you know Lucia did it?" He asked, ignoring Leonard's reflections.

"Carmen was wearing a ring when I met her. The delicacy and size of the gem caught my attention"-he sighed.

"And?"

"The ring was found under Lucia's bed."

"Oh!"

"Lucia hit Carmen with the candlestick. Felipe tried to cover the murder by pretending it was suicide,"

"So, Carmen never gave you a confession implicating her sister?"

"No, she didn't."

"But she gave you the treasure map." He inquired- "then who wrote the letter accusing Lucia?" - Leonard approached his desk and gave him a paper.

"This is about golf. You tricked her!"

"You know, Andrew, life didn't grant me a sibling; it took me some time to understand the rivalry and resentment among those two women."

"She declared it wasn't murder, but an accident."

"Half of the crimes are passionate accidents."

"Two sisters with hearts full of rancor," remarked Andy.

"Enough to destroy them." Said Leo, shivering- "Is it getting cold?"

"Ice cold!" The night covered the room with a dark ghostly air. A creepy chill came out of nowhere. Andrew stoked the fire, at that moment, he felt someone next to him -"It smells like orange and flowers," he noticed, kneeling at the fireplace.

"I don't smell anything."

"What was that?" Asked the servant jumping.

"What?"

"Someone touched my back. It felt icy cold!" He cried nervously.

"You're imagining things. We're alone." -Leonard approached the chimney. He was meditative. "I can't deny this crime had an impact on me."

"Indeed, there is an overwhelmed feeling in the castle."

"We all should be hungry for life. Hungry for a passionate existence. Make every day count with a fiery heart."

Andrew looked at him incredulously and said smiling, "Be the salt of the Earth."

"And the light of the world." Said Leo, narrowing his eyes. He took a glass and filed up to make a toast. "To remember to spread light in the darkness."

"I drink to that."

The monarch drank in one gulp and promised to stop waiting for the miraculous day when he would get rid of the burden of tedious work, "There is a reward in my duties. My life has a purpose." He noticed optimistically.

"Hail the King!"

Leo continued, "Sure, hail the king, and you…" He hit the servant in the stomach with a rolled parchment, "Don't forget your task." Then, he disappeared behind the door- "Good night."

"My task. What task? Good night to you, milord." Andy toured the room looking for the ghostly presence he felt before, but the night was quiet, and the only noise came from the crackling wood of the fireplace. *"Come on man, there's nobody here, and why do I always say yes to his commissions? Let's see what he wants now,"* he opened the rolled parchment and read:

Andrew,

You will find two sentences on my desk, read them and choose the one to be executed. Please decide as soon as possible, as I am expected to resolve the matter by midday tomorrow.

My gratitude in advance.

Leonard,

"Read the two sentences and choose one for execution," Andrew repeated, holding both edicts.

Dona Lucia Lorenzo y Gongora:

You have been charged, trial, and convicted, for your willful commission of a crime, against the crown, for the murder of Dona Carmen Lorenzo y Gongora and Don Felipe Sanchez y Hurtado.

You hereby have been sentenced in this day, to be hanged by the neck until death.

May God have mercy on your soul,

The King.

November 6th 1523, the Year of the Lord

The Kingdom of Norland.

Dona Lucia Lorenzo y Gongora

You have been charged, tried, and convicted, for your willful commission of a crime, against the crown, for the murder of Dona Carmen Lorenzo y Gongora and Don Felipe Salazar y Hurtado.

You hereby have been sentenced on this day, to live prisoner in the tower of the kingdom until the day of your death.

May God have mercy on your soul.

The King

November 6th 1523, the year of the Lord

The Kingdom of Norland.

Eighteen

A New World

"Is it your intention that I accept the fruits of piracy, Lord Norton?"- asked Leonard, seated in the middle of the audience chamber receiving tributes.

"None of my fleets are committed to acts of piracy, milord. These are nothing but treasures from expeditions to the New World" -answered Charles Norton.

"The next room is filled with members of neighbor kingdoms. They are demanding your head," warned Leo with a sharp smile.

"They are mistaken, majesty," Norton opened chests, "feast your eyes with the fortunes I have forwarded to the crown. Our ships had brought abundant wealth to the kingdom; crates of corn, cocoa, potatoes, among tons of gold. And indeed, his majesty's favorite new crop... tobacco."

"Quite a testimony, Sir Norton." Duke Chadwick finally spoke. Years had passed, and the expeditions to the New World were increasing every year. What was thought to be a barren wasteland was actually an incredible opportunity, with a fertile territory which produced exotic crops never seen before. The King couldn't complain of his good fortune, but he definitely complained of the unbearable heat of that summer. He was copiously sweating, setting in the Throne Room, full of luxurious trappings and furniture. He was inside of an outer coat with ruffled cuffs and a flamboyant suffocating cravat.

"*Bloody fashion is getting so absurd*!" He thought while drinking water from a golden cup. After a few minutes of silence he addressed the crowd, "I welcome you, and your fleets, but I warn you. I shall not tolerate intrigues in my court," he said, sinking his face in a wet towel.

"By all means, your majesty," the buccaneer bowed and disappeared in the crowd. Leo rose from the throne and nodded to the captain of the guard expecting to be free from more audiences.

"Your, Highness, the members of the Parliament, they have been waiting for hours" -informed his captain concerned.

"Can someone open the windows and allow fresh air?"

"All windows are open, your majesty."

The King sat down again. There was no way out. He had to finish with the agenda for the day.

"Who else is asking for an audience?"

"King Gustave's messengers, milord."

"From Normandia?"

"Yes, your honor."

Normandia was north of the kingdom. Legendary for its impregnable forts and courageous armies; bloodthirsty warriors that devastated their enemies, considered almost mythological heroes. Leonard's army fought for years with Normandia, until an alliance was signed between the two powerful nations, and both countries respected their territories. However, the fascinating story of his all-time enemy was not about war, but a legendary love story.

The story of King Gustave, and his wife, Felicity; the astonishing blond beauty of the North, a heated affair that bordered madness. Sonatas, poems, and plays honored the outstanding romance with Lady Sitguourd and the Viking, foreign propaganda that made Leo jealous.

Annoyed, the King made a sign to receive the visitors. Ivan, Gustave's spokesman, entered the great hall, followed by his soldiers. He was a bulky man, with rosy skin, light red hair, and small eyes wearing a long calf-length tunic and a bear fur on his back.

"Ridiculous, dressed like that in this heat!" Leo thought.

The prominent man, drenched in sweat, stopped right in front of the throne, bowed on one knee, and delivered his message, "we're here to share sonatas and poems written to celebrate the true love of our King with Lady Sitguourd."

"Oh, Hurray!" Leonard made a sign to Ivan to stand up.

"Also, it's with great pleasure that King Gustave offers the hand of his niece, Ingrid of Ahlstrom, in marriage to his highness Leonard of Norland." And Ivan displayed a painting of the beauty. Leo looked perplexed at the underrated messenger.

"Thank you. What a surprise," he smiled to the court. Some monarchs thought of Leo as an enchanted man. Many sovereigns tried to share his secret by becoming part of his family. Others made attempts to offer sisters, daughters and any lady hands available, as a possible queen for the wizard king. Leo refused one after another, for him, marriage was a matter of love, not politics.

"I shall consider this honorable proposal, and answer to his majesty shortly. Extend our gratitude to the King for his lovely poems."

Count Lyondell, Speaker of the House, approached the King, clearing his throat. He whispered in Leo's ear, "pardon, Milord. Your counselors and most of the people in the realm are loyal subjects to the Crown. We are expecting a royal wedding and an heir with enthusiasm."

Leo knew that the enemies of the Crown were multiplying every day. However, he amused himself with the rumors, and tales of his supposedly magic powers.

"The future of the realm concerns me as much as anyone, Count."-He looked at Lyondell with contempt- "The right time would arrive to celebrate a royal wedding. Now, if you excuse me, I am exhausted!" -He rose from the throne.

"Your grace." The Count bowed and dismissed the court. It was evident that Leo was losing power. Some members of the Parliament were afraid of his longevity and were in a constant struggle against him. The most powerful was the Duke of Wilton, one of Leo's few relatives.

Grouchy and tired, Leo left the room to find some relief.

The true love of Gustave and Felicity…damn their sonatas and poems…bloody bastard…Gustave is nothing but a murderer!" Leo cursed, and slammed the door of his private office.

"Talking to yourself again?' -asked Andrew amused. He was sitting on Leo's desk.

"Why are you not sweating with this bloody heat?"

"I keep my cool from body and soul."

"Do you?" Leo took his coat.

Andrew stared at him, "I don't fall prisoner of basic desires."

"I see,"

"What troubles you now?"

"Gustave from Normandia."

"Does he want to invade us again?"

"Worst. He's offering me a bride...one of his cousins, or nieces."

"What's wrong with that? I bet she's a beauty with strong thighs."

"I won't marry without love."

The squire unrolled a parchment and stared at his friend, "love only brings pain and trouble."

"Mmmm, here we go…"

"It's true; love is an absolute waste of time and energy. There's nothing better than exiting copulation without a settlement. As God commands."

"The heat is cooking your brain. I don't have time for your vein interpretation of the scriptures."

"Then, set your mind on important enterprises. "

"What's more important than love?" He said, reading some of Gustave poems.

"Here….this is an urgent letter."

"I don't think so."

"Yes, read this. It requires your immediate attention," Andy shoved a parchment into Leo's hands, and took away the poems.

 nineteen

"Your Majesty:

It pains me to inform you that your father's condition has worsened. He hasn't come out of the manor for months, and he barely leaves his own chambers these days.

I'm not sure how he has done it, but he continues to receive a steady supply of liquor, which he inevitably consumes, further worsening his condition.

I've gone as far as placing guards outside his door, but he continues to outsmart them. Recently, he got upset and dismissed all service, making me the only servant in the castle."

"I ordered double efforts to prevent him from the bloody alcohol!"- Leo held the letter in his fingers, "he always ended up finding ways."

"Your father is clever and… stubborn!" –added Andrew.

Leo continued reading:

> *"He has gone on a week-long binge and has now fallen ill, he can't recognize me anymore. I'm afraid by the time this letter reaches you it will be too late.*
>
> *Regards,*
>
> *Thomas, Steward of the Wenrial Château,*
>
> *House of BayCastle.*
>
> *July 6th, of the Year of the Lord."*

The King wadded up the letter, "his stubbornness might take his life."

The potion in Philippe's body was decaying, and the regeneration of his cells could no longer keep up with the damage made to his internal organs. Phillipe's life was at risk.

Andrew stopped reading and asked- "When shall we leave?"

"At once!"

Ghost of the Past

The fastest way to the castle was by boat.

Although there was a short journey, the young king felt consumed by anxiety, knowing that any minute his father could perish. A few hours later, the ship finished its trip, and they disembarked with urgency. Without thinking twice, Leo straddled a champagne steed sporting a shiny coat and rode aggressively to the citadel. Andrew looked as his master left, as he was barely disembarking the ship.

The road to the manor seemed like an eternity and Leo felt a warm agitation in his heart, when the small chateau slowly emerged, as he ascended uphill along the bay. Although the castle was modest in size, it had the splendor of a royal structure; the dark grey stone was grimly decorated by a gothic façade.

"There it is…Wenrial, the château where I was born, set on an island where three sea lochs meet." The sweet scent of the forest reminded him of his childhood. Tiny stained-glass windows peered through the single west tower in which Leo knew his father would be. The young king remembered how much he loved to look at the stars, in the little tower. Where he spent hours studying astronomy.

As he approached the front gates, he noticed that no servants came to aide him. He jumped off the horse, and proceeded to the front door, without even grabbing the margin of a twelve-karat silver knocker, the enormous door opened as if summoned.

"You're here, milord," an old raspy voice said.

Leo could barely recognize his father's servant. What was a usually impeccable steward had become a tired old man. It became more apparent with the years, the staff would age noticeably faster. Something that he never quite got used to. It always baffled him how his subjects would eventually be torn by time. He, however, didn't expect to find Thomas in his present state. The poor soul looked like he hadn't changed his clothes in weeks. His usually clean-cut hair was long and mangled, and his beard was unusually shabby. Leo felt a sting of guilt; perhaps Thomas was so beaten because he had been taking care of the stubborn old man for so long. Something Leo should have been doing himself. Leo read the anguish in Thomas' expression.

"Milord, is it you. Thanks to the Holy Trinity."

"Yes, Thomas, I'm here."

The servant's voice was hoarse and dim, Leo could hardly hear him.

"You're father…King Phillipe…"

"Is he dead?"

"No…no, but he's very weak, and only cries your name, milord," he said cleaning sweat from his forehead, "I don't know what to do…he refuses to be fed."

"Where is he?"

"Upstairs, in his chamber,"- Thomas took a deep breath.

"I shall convene with you later" -Leo dashed up the tower.

As soon as he opened the heavy door, a stench of liquor invaded him. He pushed aside the desire to lecture his father sternly.

Next, he approached the large oak bed where he knew his father was laying. The curtains were drawn, and he could barely see a lump of sheets moving in the rhythm of steady breathing.

He silently approached him, once he saw him, all his anger withered away. Phillipe was sleeping soundly, looking harmless and calm. This shook Leo a bit.

"Father," Leo whispered.

"Leave me alone…"

"Wake up…it's me."

"What do you want?"

"I've come to nurse you back to health."

"Let me die in peace; I don't know thee," the old man answered and turned to the other side. Leo was irritated; he grabbed his father by both arms and heaved him upwards.

"Father. Can you hear me?"

"LEONARD! SON….Is that you?"

"YES!"

Phillipe woke instantly and smiled at his son, a faint expression of happiness on his face, then in an instant, he went pale, opened his eyes in alarm, and violently plunged forward, he then got sick all over his startled son.

Leo let his father collapse back in the bed, "Oh….Phillipe!" He was covered with vomit-"What a welcoming," he mumbled, cleaning his robe.

"At least you're alive." Leo removed his clothes.

"My son is here….my only son."

"Andrew!" -Leo called- "Upstairs…I need you…" He forgot his servant was not in the manner. He took off his clothes, and for a minute, he regretted the trip and the effort. His old man had disaster written all over him, he had lost so much weight that he was almost a skeleton.

"I wondered if I would be able to stay here without getting angrier at you with every passing hour."

"Ha, ha, ha. I've missed you too."

"Where in the hell is the creep? Andrew!" He shouted, as he threw his dirty clothes to the floor.

"Uh…I'm thirsty"-The old man was in pain. Leo went over to his father and tried to help him clean up.

At this point, the father was mumbling half asleep something about, "Son, before I die. You ought to know…."

"Shh…Let me clean you, papa."

Thomas appeared at the room, an utter expression of confusion in his eyes, "Milord, did you call me?"

"Tell my servant, to bring a clean set of clothes, and soup for my father."

The steward looked around, lifted his shoulders, and stared at Leo, inquiring if the master was also drunk. "There's nobody in the castle but us."

"HELL, I'LL BE DAMN!" and he remembered Andrew was at the docks with the luggage.

Twenty

"How do I love thee? Let me count the ways
I love thee to the depth and breadth, and height,
My soul can reach"
- Elizabeth Barrett Browning

The love story of Gustave and Felicity happened not long ago. Felicity, the owner of a fascinating combination of beauty and brightness, met warrior Gustave at a party in her native Skyen. Both victims of instant attraction made their acquaintance on a cold winter night. Perspicuous Felicity decided that Gustave would surrender to her charms and wish for a rapid marriage. Days after the encounter, deep in the woods, inside a cabin, two fearsome witches were working on a spell.

"The heart of the warrior shall be yours, and none else's. It is Balk's wish…our god,"-said an old woman placing a potion with ceremonial movements into Felicity's hands.

"Drink my child, and the lips of the warrior will remain impregnated with your kisses. Every kiss of yours. It will be vital for him. As urgent as water to fish, and as necessary as air to his lungs."

Felicity closed her eyes and drank from the steamy goblet.

"Soon, you'll be his wife. Later his crown queen." said the sorcerer while throwing herbs into a boiling cauldron.

"No, mother, you don't understand… He is not a king; he's a warrior!"

"Well, we can fix that, can't we?" The older woman laughed darkly.

"How?"

"My child…we have ways…" She added quickly, "You have to convince him."

"Convince him of what?"

"The mighty warrior was born to rule… to be King… a mighty King! You see a man of his size, his strength, and his… brains."

"Yes, I love him….and I want the best for him."

"Then show him the way, lift him. He ought to be the new ruler of these lands."

"But how?

"By ….killing… the King, my darling," answered the sinister woman.

"Is that possible?"

"Everything is possible, watch and learn from your mother."

The cauldron flooded the cabin with thick black smoke.

The darkness of the night penetrated the hearts of the women, who surrendered to the shadows.

The Encounter

The vomit incident certainly didn't aid his father's cause.

Afraid of losing his temper, Leo asked Thomas to help him, and lend him some of his clean clothes. Both men cleaned Philippe and the room.

"When did you arrive, son?" -his father was finally sober.

"Today, about noon."

"Yes, milord….past noon," noticed Tomas.

"I'm happy to see you, son. Glory to the Providence that brought you to me, before I die" -he was holding a piece of bread with trembling hands. He looked at his son half-conscious and nodded with a sense of guilt as his weak body was not able to stay awake for long periods of time.

"Son," he stopped and looked at Leo with tenderness. "Have I told you that you have her smile?"

"Yes, father…many times."

The old man closed his eyes and nodded his head, "she was the love of his life."

Leo smiled and continued spoon feeding him, "come on, dad finish your soup."

"I'm so grateful you are here.... So grateful. Where are we, son?"

"This is Wenrial, the Château. "

"You confined me against my will!"

"No, dad. This exile was your idea."

"Perhaps, " said Phillip with watery eyes, "but, you ought to know, your mother is calling me, son."

"Please, father. I need you. You're everything I have."

"Yes…yes, my child. I know. Now I need to rest. Leave me alone." Phillipe said, and in a question of minutes, fell asleep.

"He looks helpless, like a child," noticed Leo, covering him with clean sheets.

"Milord, thank you for answering my letter."

"Thomas, it's me who has to thank you for taking care of my old man," Leo patted him on the back, "I should spend more time with him."

"He'll be alright; he finally ate."

"Is Andrew back?"

"No yet, milord."

"What is taking him so long?"

Leo took the stairs, and he heard a firm dog bark. It was Saxon, his father's Labrador. "Hey! How are you, old boy?" The dog wagged his tail to greet him. Leo hugged the dog with enthusiasm, "Yes, friend. Let's go out. See if Andrew is within sight."

They made their way to the shore. The King was calmer, however sad. A lonely feeling overwhelmed him with the thought of losing his father. The mighty warrior was a sick alcoholic.

"He's as miserable as I am, perishing in a gilded cage, and he doesn't acknowledge the pain he's causing me," he thought and ran to the shore with the dog next to him.

"This outfit is so comfortable," he noticed touching his chest. *"Astonish!"* -He felt ungrateful; he had it all, immortality, wealth, power. A life of privileges yet, he was alone. There was no companion to share his fortune. Sometimes, he allowed the fantasy of an ordinary existence. He was convinced that wealth and bitterness were somehow connected.

He stopped and turned to see his father's window in the tower.

"Poor old man, he loved my mother so much. I wonder if I ever feel something so deep, so intimate and close," he stared at the horizon as if he wished for a miracle.

"I've been waiting so long...." –he told Saxon who was licking his hand.

"Are you trying to cheer me up? You want to play, don't you?" The doggy waved his tale and his loving eyes answered Leo, who threw a stick on the shore.

"Here boy, bring back the stick."

Saxon ran delighted, and Leo drew a smile, for a moment he felt the freedom he lost in childhood; he stared away to the castle and realized that the solid structure was more than a vague memory of his past. Saxon returned proudly with the stick in the snout.

"Good boy, here catch it again and this time bring me true love!"

The evening was winding down. A warm sunset colored the horizon orange with red shadows. Flashes of sparking light jumped on the ocean as gemstones. Summer haze and fog covered the horizon, and from it, emerged a living goddess figure. Walking along with a horse. The most majestic woman rose to the eyes of the monarch.

Tall, blond with delicate milky skin, she was wearing a long light blue dress that made her glimmer as a heavenly vision. The glamorous, dazzling beauty could only possibly be...

"An angel!" He thought, as he cast eyes on the silky figure.

"Are you human?" He asked, perplexed as she crossed his way in silence.

"Do I look like a ghost to you?" She answered with disdain.

"No! Don't get me wrong…I thought you were an angel." He replied ashamed, and sincerely.

"Don't use cheap flattery with me, milord." She stared at him, causing him a warm sensation.

"If you have heard that line before, it's because it contains truth."

She smiled slightly and said-"You're kind. However, there is no heavenly condition in a trouble heart."

"Do you have misfortunes?"

"Who's free of worries on this Earth?"

He nodded.

"The only thing left for us, is to be kind to each other," she said.

Leo noticed her pupils dilated, as he took her hand.

"Milady, please allowed me to introduce myself."

She moved away and said, "I'm sorry. I must go."

"I beg your pardon."

"You see, gentleman, I'm promised in marriage. I can talk to strangers," she retorted.

"Because you're engaged?"

"That's what I said."

"Remarkable! Then you must be in love."

A sad expression covered her face as she walked on the shore gently, then she asked, "I can't say. How to know when you're in love?"

"*Love needs no reason. It's a wild passion that burns inside.*" He recited.

She mounted her horse, and added, "*Divine flame that drowns the soul,*"

"*And captures the mind,*" he completed the poem. "Forgive my pretension, please tell me your name, before you leave."

"Milord, please disregard this encounter, as the gentlemen you are," and she rode away on her horse. Leo trotted pathetically behind her.

"Don't leave without telling me your ..."

"Grace?"

"Yes…. your name,"

She rode vigorously and shouted at him from a distance.

"I just told you!"

Twenty one

The Lady at the Shore

"Lady Grace, milord. The granddaughter of the Archduke of ScottWinds." Tom said while serving dinner.

"I know the Archduke, but I never saw the lady.

"She is the youngest of three sisters. Daughters of Lord McConnery."

"So, she has lineage!" Noticed Leo eating soup. His eyes sparkled.

"Yes, ended, milord."

"She's a woman owner of a magnificent…"

"Beauty!" The servant added.

"More that beauty, she has a natural elegance,"

"She is a dazzling lady and a kind soul," said Thomas.

"Who is she engaged to?"

"Baron Martin Watters. A middle-aged landlord facing bankruptcy."

"A gentleman in need of a dowry," guessed Leo.

"Precisely. He intends to recover his state."

"Thomas, I need to see her again."

"Recently, she has developed an obsession for the castle. She comes almost every afternoon," Thomas informed with awe.

"Why does she do that?"

"To paint it."

"Does she come inside?"

"No….you see, her family. If your excuse me, milord."

"Say it!... They hate me."

"They fear you and king Phillipe."-He affirmed with sorrow.

"So, why does she paint the castle?"

"I don't know. She's been painting the manor since the announcement of her engagement."

"When is her wedding?"

The servant was chewing, "I'm not sure, a couple of weeks, I guess."

"Weeks?" Leo stopped eating. The sun was hiding. The ocean breeze refreshed the manor pleasantly. Leo got silent, reflective. Walked around the table and lit his pipe. He had to act, fast. "Thomas…" He finally spoke.

"Yes, milord."

"You stay with my father on this side of the castle. I'll remain on the east wing. I don't want anyone around me. I'll come personally to get food and essentials."

"By all means, milord." The servant stood up and bowed.

"I want your complete discretion on this issue. Ah, and I need more of these comfortable clothes."

"As you wish, Majesty."

"Remember, you shall mention this to no one. Understood!"

"Yes, milord," Thomas bowed again.

Homecoming

Andrew walked uphill towards *Wenrial.* He cursed Leo under his breath for leaving him behind, as he wished to see Phillipe too. King Phillipe was, at one time, the only father figure he had when growing in the castle. After some hours in the town, the squire completed a list of supplies and hired a handful of servants willing to work with Thomas. The door of the kitchen opened suddenly, and Andrew entered.

"Ah...Thomas old man." The two servants hugged.

"My good friend...ha...ha... Be welcome!"

"Here!" Andrew put a sack on the table and said, "I brought supplies for your pantry."

"You got so much. Sweet the moments rich in blessings," said Thomas, who started unpacking.

"Ah, good friend...I was wondering what happened to you." Said the servant staring at two women.

"How is King Philippe?" Andrew asked and took his gloves off.

"Better," Informed Thomas.

"He ate, and he's sleeping now." Added Leo, who entered the room smoking his pipe.

"I want to see him."

"You wait; he had enough for today," noticed Leo.

"By all means. I brought you help, Thomas." Andrew said, offering a seat to the young maids. "Meet Katerine, an excellent cook and Selda your new housekeeper."

"Welcome to Wenrial Château, maladies," Thomas said, feeling lucky.

"Gentlemen, it's been a long day. I need some rest," –said Leo waking to the door, "you two catch up and don't stay up late. I need all the help I can get; this place is a disgrace." He said, disappearing with a candlestick in his hand, while Thomas smiled at the ladies revealing his rotten teeth.

Twenty two

"Stars hire your fires,
Let no light see my black and deep desires."
- Shakespeare.

Quietly, being careful of not making noise, two shadows were walking inside a dark castle. A bulky middle-aged man and his young wife were dressed in black. The doubtful man stopped as they arrived at the end of a hall; the woman looked sideways and made a signal to continue to the royal chamber.

From a cloth bag, she pulled out a shining silver dagger- a present from her mother. Felicity put the dagger in her husband's hand in complete silence. Both entered the chamber; she looked inquisitive to Gustave and whispered.

"Come on, it's Balk's command!" –and they beckon along with the plan. The tall man looked at his monarch, helplessly asleep in his bed. They already had diverted all the guards; so, the remaining task was nailing the knife in the jugular of the King.

An easy job for the brave warrior during war times, yet complicated task for that night. The man in the bed trusted him, made him his best warrior, his friend. Gustave looked at his wife and moved his head; he was not able to do it.

"There is no time….do it now!" -she ordered and grabbed his hand to stab the victim herself, plunging the dagger deep into his neck.

Gustave took a deep breath and said to himself, "this is my destiny; it is the god's will. I shall be king" – and sliced the neck of the sleeping man to stain his hands with royal blood. The room became darker, the night deep and silent. The eyes of the couple were full of exciting greed. Both ran back to their chamber; Felicity interrupted the silence with hysterical laughter. She approached him and kissed his lips.

"You are king now, king of Iceland. You fulfill your destiny!"

She started removing her blood-drenched clothes and cleansed her husband's crimson-stained hands. Once naked, they stared at each other; she motioned him to join her in their marriage bed. Overwhelming desire burned in their skins. Lust indulged them, and the couple made love passionately that night.

Memories

And so it happened that my youth passed smoothly as leaves carried by the wind; like waves that melt into the ocean, like shooting stars loaded with innocent dreams.

A big splash of water came out of Phil's bath. Leo had taken himself the task of caring for his father. He rubbed his back silently, still dazed by the empty ale bottle that found its way to his bedside. The old man cackled happily, "I'm not drunk, son. I'm only celebrating your visit after ages…ha..ha..ha" -He laughed and caressed Leo's face.

"Apparently, you feel well enough, and we can't stop drinking, can we?"

"I drink because I'm celebrating. A glorious celebration of seeing my son again,"

"Sure excuses for drinking are a million, aren't they?"

"Are you upset, my boy?" –he squeezed Leo's cheeks, "God, I love my son!" -the old man collapsed on his bed and fell asleep.

"I will not succeed, Andrew, this is stronger than my will."

"I searched everywhere; there is no more alcohol in the castle."

"It may be too late."

"Let him sleep. I'll feed him when he wakes up. Go downstairs and have some breakfast."

After he ate, Leo strolled through the castle. The state of the property was unfortunate, covered in dust and spider webs. Piles of chests were cornered in almost every room. A great feeling of melancholy invaded him, and childhood memories crashed like waves on a stormy night. Suddenly, memories stopped. And unintentionally, he focused on the image of the angelical woman…Grace. *Could it be love at first sight?* -or an intense lust he had not experienced before. Whatever it was, he had to see her again.

Unaware, he stood in front of what in the past was, his parent's chamber. He entered the room warily and recognized a small cabinet used by his mother. Indescribable joy and a tender feeling came over as he passed his hand on the old wood.

"Why to dwell upon memories?"-he thought and tried to exit the room, but her portrait caught his eye. *"Mother!"*-he cried, moved. He ran back to the cabinet and opened the small drawers, as he was looking for a message from her.

He found several letters written by his father. The documents mentioned Uncle Henry, and confirmed the strategy to assume the throne and remove the Crown from his own brother. Suddenly, Leo's eyes settled on a letter addressed to his grandmother.

"Providence has blessed us with the most beautiful child ever seen in these lands; a big, healthy, boy.

We finally know the peace and happiness of producing an heir to the Throne. After many painful attempts in which we lost one baby, this child is filling our lives with joy and blessings.

As soon as my wife feels stronger, we will travel to meet you.

By now, all our love and care are directed to our treasure from heaven, our miracle baby boy, Leonard."

"Wow! Memories were just" -Leo was born and raised in that castle until the age of seven when they relocated, so his father could take over the Kingdom. They say people are created equal. That's true! The mystery, the enigma, is why people are born in arbitrary circumstances.

Who set the pre-birth plan? Who decides who will be born in a privilege cradle or in an indigent home?

"I was born blessed"-he reflected. He couldn't be more grateful for the perfect design of his birth; the place and the status quo. Nevertheless, the real reason to feel thankful was the memories of the unconditional love his parents felt for each other. Love that wrapped him tenderly during his childhood.

The rest of the afternoon, he continued hunting for memories. When the sunset and the first stars began to blink on the velvet sky, he decided to check on his father. The former sovereign was eating again, and color had returned to his pale face. Within a few hours, a feeling of hope dwelled in the castle, as everybody felt enthusiastic about Phil's recovery. After supper, Leo decided to take a walk on the beach. The summer sky was splashed with millions of stars that illuminated his path. A soft breeze from the ocean cleared his mind, as he paid particular attention to the sound of the waves breaking at his feet. Walking on the beach, there was only one thought on his head…*"Grace, yes, I can feel you…You'll be mine."*

Twenty three

Mesmerized Desire

"Remarkable painting, milady. You captured the feeling of this place," said Leonard coming out from bushes.

"Oh, my God, where did you come from?" The lady wasn't aware of his presence.

"Forgive me if I scared you. I just saw you from the castle."

"I'm not scared. It's… not proper to be here alone with you. I shall go."

"Allow me to introduce myself…I'm Andrew, the new steward of the castle, at your service milady." He bowed.

"Grace of ScottWings," she dropped a curtesy.

"I was saying you capture the feeling of the picturesque building."- He held the picture.

"*Wenrial* is an exquisite structure," she said proudly of her effort-"This building contains a perfect geometric symmetry, and placed on a ridge, gives it a distinctive impression."

"It was built as a fortress in the year 1265. A curtain-wall castle. It's small, but it has served its purpose."

"Certainly, it does," she blushed-"It's the home of the evilest and most powerful hierarchy in the continent. A family known for their immense ambition," said Grace with passion.

"Indeed?" He smiled- "I presume, you don't participate in the King's court much. Have you been presented to the court?" -He asked her, a bit intimidated by her apparent disgust.

"No. My oldest sister was presented to court some years ago. We travel to see the King. I was a child. We never visit the King's court again."

"Why so?"

"My family knows King Leonard as an evil man, willing to live an eternal life to feed his insatiable appetite for carnal pleasures," Grace retorted- "My father kept us safe here."

"Oh, are you certain of such rumors?"

She leaned over and whispered. "They said the enchanted master of this castle, King Philippe, is the owner of a tormented soul."

"And they might be correct, milady," he answered sadly- "Then why to bother? What is your attraction to this place?"

She blushed. "That is what I been wondering all this time. A sinister magnet that attracts me to paint this castle. It's a deep feeling that I cannot control," she took her book of sketches and held it close to her chest. "Perhaps, suppositions are true."

"About what?"

"They said…passion is stronger than virtue. And most of our passions tend to be sinful."

"Really, but what is a sin?" -He asked, expecting her answer.

"A sin is something that will damage our relationship with God."

"God knows our nature," Leonard smiled, charmed.

"Yes, HE does." She looked at him with interest and asked, "So, Andrew, are you new in town?"

"Yes, I'm working at the Chateau, but I don't know anybody."

"Well, you know me, now."

"I don't want to be impertinent, but I've been wondering about your engagement. You don't seem satisfy."

"I must be nervous; the marriage will be celebrated soon."

"How soon?"

"Three weeks."

"Perhaps I'm insolent, but…I asked the other day and asked again. Are you in love?" He stood close to her, making her uncomfortable.

"My hand in marriage is my father's affair. I have a devoted love for my father." And she rushed to mount her horse.

"Then, we have something in common. My only true concern is the welfare of my father," he continued trying pathetically to keep her longer-"You see, he's the only member of my family alive…and he's ill."

"Oh, I'm sorry to hear that, I'll say some prays for his recovery."

"I'll appreciate it very much, milady."

"You have a good day, gentleman."

"No, wait…So, you spoke of your love for your father, but you didn't say anything about your fiancé?"

Drops of rain fell, and a couple landed on Grace's cheeks. She wiped the water with her fingers; Leo wasn't sure it was rain drops as her expression was somber. She walked next to her horse where she gathered all her tools together. Leo held her horse rains and said, "Why to marry without love?"

"It's my duty."

"Talk to your father, explain."

"There is nothing to talk about. My father's will is mine, and I shall make any sacrifice for my family. Wouldn't you do the same?"

"You have no idea. You're brave and loyal. So, I like it!"

She stepped back and asked, "Are you married, Andrew?"

"I was many years ago. I'm a widow now."

"I'm sorry. I have to go, or my paintings will be ruined."

"I just want to be with thee; I need to tell you, so much." He said tenderly, thinking he needed her in his life.

"You know Andrew, there is something I should confess."

"I'm all ears."

"Since I was a little girl, I've always known. Deep in my heart, I was sure…"-She paused.

"Speak freely."

"I was sure, I will experience true love in this life; I know is my destiny," she said, and her face glowed.

"True love doesn't exist, milady," he said sadly-"It's only a tale for troubadours and dreamers."

"Then, milord, what would the world be without troubadours and dreamers?"

"Please, come with me inside the castle. You will be wet, your paintings ruined."

"No. I can't go inside."

He moved close to her and said, "I shall protect you… from any evil…from any wicked man. I'll keep you save…forever." And he held her hands. She felt a surge down her spine, he noticed her reaction and whispered in her ear- "Show me, there is true love."

Grace's pupils opened wild; her heart raced, a chemistry bomb exploded between them.

She took her horse and jumped on it. Next, she turned to him- "Gentleman, I might accept your invitation and go inside the castle, one of these days."

"Then, I shall wait for you tomorrow." He stared at her- "I'll be honored to take supper with, milady," and he bowed.

Ada

Grace talked about Leo all day, "I don't know if I should go, nanny; I've just met him."

"No child. Your place is here, in the manner," answered Ada, a middle age woman.

"I know, but he is so…handsome and eloquent. He makes me feel…important!" She recalled with a dreamy smile.

"If your fiancée were to hear about that man…"

"Andrew,"

"Anyway, he's a stranger. There is no word about him."

"I just told you. He's the new steward of the castle," Grace said absent- mindedly, "and when he looks at me with those flirtatious eyes."

"Hmm, child. I know he fires your heart," said Ada, folding sheets looking at Grace with a furry face.

"Oh, my God, you don't know how," Grace bit her lower lip.

"Yes, I have an idea."

"His provocative grey eyes have a delightful combination of lust and admiration. Maybe, I'm feeling lust too!" She giggled, "I don't know, I never felt so excited before."

"A servant, milady? He's a servant to the old king. You are engaged to a Baron."

"A man in need of my fortune more than my love? Soon, I'll be miserably married to the Baron of Watters," Grace sighed and collapsed face up on her bed. She lost her stare on the intricately decorated roof, which it was hand-painted with pink and white cherubim. She admitted how ridiculous the thought of falling in love was, but she reluctantly felt that way, and she embraced it. Her nanny stared at her and felt sad. She knew her young mistress was right, the Baron would never make her happy. Enabling a secret relationship like this would be risky, but also the last chance for her lady to feel love, even, if it was for a few days before her wedding.

"Oh, nanny, nanny…what's happening to me. I can't take him from my head!" The young lady twirled in her bed.

Ada loved her like a daughter, and the single thought of her being miserable in a loveless marriage broke her heart. She sat next to her -"What if you go? Only for one single time."

"Do you think it will be possible?"

"There is a way, milady." Ada answered and held Grace's hands.

"But my father?"

"He'll never find out."

"But if he…"

"We'll take him with a grain of salt," Ada said and ran to her mistress's wardrobe to choose a gown. Inspiration came to her like a lighting, "Damn the Baron, the devil dwell within the wood."

"What are you saying? I can't hear you."

"We take our changes, and this can be yours, my child." She exclaimed, knocking on the wood of furniture. Next, she presented a dress. "This gown makes you blue eyes look deep like the ocean."

"But… nanny!"

"Come on, I'll dress you up. The gentleman is waiting. I'll arrange a carriage and find an excuse for you at supper. Gussy up."

"Milord, there is something in you that attracts me like a magnet, and makes me want you."

"Milady, you awake my deepest desire. You are something that I urgently need."

Twenty Four

A Growing Tree

Ocean scent perfumed the castle, and the room lite with candles where the young Romeo settled down his secret date. Away from the rest of the world. Leonard was thrilled when he saw Grace getting off the carriage.

"Welcome to Wenrial Château, milady."

"Finally, I'll see the castle from inside."

"Nothing to fear….allow me," he said, offering his arm and leading the way. She felt excited when they crossed a couple of halls and finally arrived at a meticulously decorated room. The pale moonlight revealed the lady's beauty.

"Flowers, wine…candles," she took a grape from a fruit plater, and caressed her lips with it, "are we playing the seduction game, Andrew?"

"What else can be done on a night like this?" He held her hand and offered a chair. Ada was right. Grace's dress was exquisite and highlighted her eyes.

"Your deep blue eyes feel my heart with joy as a water spring" –Leo noticed -"It would be a sin not to have them close to me forever."

Grace stared at him and smiled, "Andrew, don't be mistaken, I'm not looking for romance."

"No, milady. Romance already found us. Allow me to show you what I prepared for the occasion."

"A feast?" She asked incredulously.

"A surprise," said Leo proudly as he uncovered plates with; Garden Salad, Roast Duck with Plumbs, Cauliflower Cheese, and for desert Summer Pudding. I hope these dishes are to your liking."

"Everything looks splendid."

"My pleasure," Leonard served her with enthusiasm. He worked in the kitchen all day, with the help of the maids who also thought he was a servant. The couple ate, drank, and laughed. Grace was definitely fun and easy-going, "this meal is one of the best I had ever had. You're talented, Andrew," she cleaned her mouth, satisfied.

"I'm honored, milady." He answered, and a gratified smile peeked on his face.

"It's close in here…." She said opening her fan.

"Let's go outside." He took her into a garden.

"I was afraid you wouldn't come to my private function, after all the efforts in the kitchen."

"How to ignore such a cordial invitation?"

"Grace, I…"He got closer to her.

She stopped him, "You're aware of my settlement, I had a splendid time but is getting late, and I better leave," she walked away, but he grabbed her by her waist.

"Thy sweet disdain breaks this man into pieces… "-He recited.

*"Drown my doubt, struggled my fear,"*she continued the poem.

"Promise me thy kiss and set me free," he kissed her with passion.

"No…Andrew…" She whispered asking for more. They kissed again "I can't, the Baron…"

"Please, don't talk about the Baron. Not tonight."

He made a tender caress on her face, and her perfumed body made him experience a deep desire, "I want to take care of you."

"And who will take care of you, milord?" She walked away from him and stopped at a big tree at the end of the patio.

"The other day, you asked me to show you, true love," she touched the trunk with her back, "tell me what you see?" She asked.

"You!"

"Can you perceive God's hand in his creation?" She touched the trunk.

"Do you mean the tree?"

"God is the source of love; the type of love without expectations, generous and kind."

He looked at her intrigued. "Let's go back to the tree."

"Look closer… what can you tell me about this trunk?"

"It's big," he said, getting closer to her.

"Big and strong. It's the foundation."

"Go on, please," he was glancing at her.

"The trunk gives shape and strength. It sustains the branches that are growing around him." –She smiled- "The branches provide a refreshing shade."

"Let me guess," he was enjoying the metaphor, "men are the trunks, right?" He asked flirtatiously.

"Correct! A woman in love grows as freely as these leaves. The leaves dance with the music of their love and bend but never break because the spirit of a woman is unbreakable."

"I agreed."

"Their love gives birth to perfume flowers that bloomed among them, making every day a new experience to be cherished."

"True love!" He whispered.

"Are you listening, milord?" She asked.

"To every word you say."

"When the season is appropriate, fruits grow in the tree, making it part of a circle, like the sing of the birds that live in the tree."

"Remarkable," he notice thoughtfully, "how did you…?"

She covered his lips with her fingers; then she whispered. "Trunk and branches are connected in many ways…from inside. They are two, yet one!"

"Don't stop. I'm excited," his desire was burning, but she pushed him away, "this tree didn't grow instantly, it took time…years, to become what is today. Days of sun and water, winter, and cold; care and love. Together they defeated calamities because together, they multiply their value, and protect each other.

"Wow!"

"True love is not a temporary emotion or a passing feeling but a lifestyle. So, do you dare to witness true love; can you feel the tender shadow of this tree?"

"It's magic, and good," he said in awe.

"Is honest," she added.

"Unpretentious, and kind."

"Is faithful and brighter than the sun!"-she said when he held her by the waist and kissed her again. Grace felt an ecstasy in her body.

"Stay…."

"I can't"

"I want to play you music, sing you songs, dance…." He held her in his arms, completely mesmerized. They kissed again and again; the time disappeared.

Everything disappeared; it was only the two lovers and the silence of the night. He interrupted the moment to advise her-"You should tell your father, you don't love the Baron" - Leo was serious and grabbed her hand. Then he muttered in her ear -"Stay with me….be mine…" -He said, feeling emotions as a skyrocket.

"NO!" -She cried and felt her heart beat rapidly.

He got upset, "I command you to stay!"

"I beg your pardon?"-She pulled him away-"Who do you think you are?"

The King didn't answer and let her run to the door. Next, he reverted and ran after her, "Please forgive me. I was carried by emotion…"

"Milord, you've mistaken me for somebody else."-She got in her carriage and blushed with rage. "I don't provide that type of service!"

"No, no…I made a mistake…I enjoy your company very much."

"Good night, and thank you for the supper."

He jumped into the carriage- "Don't leave me, allowed me to serenade you. Take pity on me. Let me pick up my guitar and …"

"Andrew, forget the serenade. My father will shoot you!" She whipped the horses.

"Then come back tomorrow. Paint the castle, paint the tree. Paint me!"

"Why?" She stopped abruptly.

He jumped from the carriage and said sincerely. "Because I'm afraid you just changed my life, forever."

Connections

Everybody in the castle was engaged in the difficult mission of Phil's re-hab. During the mornings, Leo was with his father. He was in charge of his medicines, his breakfast, and a therapy to recover the circulation on his legs. They finally have time to share long-held family secrets and engaged in conversations they never had before.

"So…tell me again, son…what's the name of this mysterious lady?"

"Grace, father. She is the daughter of Lord McConnery.

"Oh…yes…the youngest daughter."

"That's right!"

"You said… her grandfather was the Archduke of ScottWinds."

"Elwood!"

"He died five years ago, right?"

"More than five, maybe ten or eleven…but who's counting years?"

"Not me…not us…ha ha ha!"-Phillipe felt joyful-"So, let's go back to the lady. When you would see her again?"

"We meet every afternoon, here in the castle."

"You are in love. I can see the emotion reflected in your eyes."

"I'm crazy for her. She is warm, funny, candid..."

"Does she love you?"

"Yes!"

"Marry her, son. I want you to be happy."

"I want to marry her, and I want you…to live with us."

"Then, bring her to my presence; I want to meet her. Give you my blessings." Leo smiled.

At last, he was at peace, he found time to be with his father, and Phillipe was proud of him. The old man accomplished the promise, he made to himself of being sober the last days of his life. For the first time, in many years, there was some energy, a connection between the two men, as never before. Phillipe told his son family stories he never shared.

Secrets he kept in his lonely heart for many years. Leonard felt admiration for his old man and wished they hadn't wasted so much time away from each other. The young sovereign couldn't hold his feeling and embraced his weak father in his arms. "I love you, papa." The old King smiled painfully and answered,

"I love you too, my son. Thank you for being here. Thank you for having mercy on an old man."

Ridge Tavern

On the other side of the castle, the rest of the service turned the filthy place into the majestic state it used to be. After weeks of hard work, Andrew and Thomas were exhausted and boring.

Mead and ale were not available anywhere. It was when Thomas convinced his friend to go for a drink at the village tavern. The men were looking for a moment to unwind from the pressure. The Ridge, as it had been called, was a small place where gentlemen could find booze and female company. Thomas was well acquainted with the place and Leonard didn't oppose to a well-deserved dissipation for his friends. It was a Wednesday when the sun was setting, and the two friends arrived at The Ridge. They ordered two drinks and sat at a table in the corner of the room.

"Here we are, my friend."

"I remember this place. It hasn't changed."

"Not a bit, cheers for this joyful reunion." Said Tom, who was holding a jar of beer, when a big man approached them and interrupted. He asked for Andrew.

"I'm Andrew. Who is asking for my acquaintance?" He responded with curiosity. The man took Andrew by his shoulder and threatened him -"I'm the Baron of Watters, and Lady Grace is my fiancée. Keep away from my future wife."

Andrew thought the Baron was a madman; he removed his hands from his clothes, pulled out his sword, and shouted, "I've never seen your lady, and I have no intention whatsoever to thee."

The Baron reacted and pulled out his sword too, "there are rumors of you seeing her secretly in the castle." Andrew blushed with anger.

"That is a lie, defamation. Defend yourself, gentleman!"

Thomas made a quick move, grabbed his chair in the air to hit Watters, who fell to the floor unconscious. The servant pushed Andrew away and shoved him to the back exit.

They mounted their horses and rode away.

Hale the King

Gustave became a wicked ruler of Iceland, he was a tyrant with a dubious heart and a guilty soul. Soon, every member of his court turned into suspicious enemy for his weak mind.

At night, he could not sleep; he spent hours furiously writing the names of possible traitors, rebels to his throne, and one by one, he eliminated almost all the names of his list, except one. Leonard King of Norland.

"You cannot continue killing your people," claimed his wife hysterically, "it seems that you are not able to trust anybody anymore."

"No, woman, I can't," he replied, cleaning the blood of his last victim.

"You're mad, insane… the blood of Iceland will remain on your conscience." She shouted hysterically.

"And in yours too." He threatened her with the knife.

"Yes, go ahead. Kill me, kill everybody and go to hell!" She shouted.

"One day, I will, witch. I will finish you too, and there will be no more secrets to keep, and no more complaints to hear."

Twenty Five

"My child, I cannot lie to your father anymore," said Ada, concerned.

"Tell him... I'm making company to any of my sisters."

"You promised me not to see him again, but the stranger had sent a carriage every afternoon," said the servant helping her lady with her dress.

"I need to see him, talk to him."

"About what? You've already delayed your marriage."

"I would end this relationship tonight, nanny. I promise you."

"No...you won't, milady and you know it-"Ada exclaimed while combing Grace's hair- "Your wedding with the Baron is next Saturday. You shall see Andrew no more."

"Oh, nanny, don't talk to me like that, please," she kissed Ada.

"Don't be late, and tell the servant farewell….for good!"

Grace jumped into a carriage hidden in the woods and waved with her handkerchief to her nanny. The young lady was overwhelmed by strong emotions. Her marriage day was getting closer, and she was out of excuses to postpone the event.

"My child will end in a convent if she continues challenging her father." Thought Ada staring at the carriage disappearing in the horizon.

Leonard was head over heels for Grace. He was convinced that she was meant to be his queen. He couldn't imagine life without her.

"My wedding is in four days, Andrew. It's time to say farewell."

"Do you really think I'll let you marry another man?"

"My father would never give us his blessing."

"Then, we elope and do a secret marriage."

"You can't be serious."

"Why not?"

"Elope, where? This is my home."

"Dear," he stared at her -"If together, we are at home." He kissed her hand and asked. "We cannot be apart anymore, can we?"

She blushed and said nervously, "in that case, I need to pick up some things. I can use my wedding dress and..."

"Alright, darling, but there's a confession I have to make."

"If it is about money…"

"It's not money…you know, I am not an ordinary servant, I am…" He hesitated for a minute, he was afraid of her reaction.

She covered his lips, "I love you, Andrew, nothing else matters."

"We have to be cautious. At the slightest suspicion, your father might lock you at the manor."

Grace nodded.

"You stay here tonight." Leo got excited, "Oh, Grace… I need to love you." Leo said and took her in his arms.

Grace resisted him and exclaimed, "If you really love me, you wait. You can't compromise my virtue, not in this place." Leonard agreed. He ran his hands through his head, trying to cool off, then reached for a glass of wine.

"Good….good…we'll wait. You can rest in my chamber tonight." He took her to his room and kissed her goodnight.

"Tomorrow we'll be husband and wife." His heart was pounding, their mouths met with hunger. He kissed her neck, "Lord I can't stop myself…you're mine, Grace." He whispered.

She closed her eyes; it was too late. Her resistance was conquered. He carried the lady in his arms and placed her on the bed, tenderly. The moon disappeared, allowing the shining stars to drench the sky. The couple continued caressing and kissing until the deep silence of the night transported them. Soon they were on the bed naked, Grace was unable to resist her hunger for the fascinating man who was taking her with love, as she allowed herself to get lost in his arms with passion. Their bodies became one. Leonard awoke Grace's senses and fed her soul and body.

The King's heart was overwhelmed with joy, he reached heaven for seconds, in the arms of his soul mate. Grace could hardly breathe. She was submerged in love, for the man holding her next to his heart.

She had problems to conceiving that a servant was so masculine, self-confident, and regal. *"There is something majestic in all of him"* - She thought.

They kissed again, and he couldn't stop loving her for the second time. After some hours, they woke up before dawn. She hurried to the carriage. She knew then she belonged to him.

"Go back and pack the essentials. Talk to no one. God be with you"-He exclaimed.

"I shall come back, love," she answered convinced, as the carriage disappeared into the woods. The love emerging from them was contagious. The sun was brighter. Everything was natural and easy. He was a different man, and his lady loved him in return. The emotion was bright, mutual, and wonderfully mesmerizing.

Virtue

Ada was waking visible afflicted into Phil's castle. Her face was red, and she was sweating copiously. She knocked at the back door, and felt the hit of the morning. She dried her sweat with her apron and began to curse.

"Thomas, where is Andrew?" She asked when the servant opened the door.

"Ada, what are you doing here?"

"I said, I'm looking for Andrew."

"He's having breakfast in the kitchen."

The small, fat woman ran into the kitchen and asked, "where is milady, Grace of Scottwinds?"

"Who? I don't know."

"Get ready to confront her father. I request an explanation of your recent behavior."

"What are you talking about?"

"Milady, didn't sleep in her bed last night!"

"Who are you?"

"Ada, Lady Grace's nurse maid."

Thomas nodded his head in affirmation.

"I'm tired of repeating myself. I don't know any mistress called Grace," he answered, and shrugging his shoulders, pressing a wet towel to his head.

The small nanny approached him and slapped his face saying- "My lordship, won't take any humiliation; he shall ask for a satisfaction to restore his honor."

"What's wrong with this woman?"

"I'm warning you….be prepare for a duel, milord." Ada exclaimed.

"Are you threatening me, old witch?"

"Curse you! And all the men of this wicked castle. You are not gentlemen, but damned wizards." And she sprinted out.

Andrew looked at Thomas and asked him- "What's going on here? Who's the crazy bitch?"

Thomas replied with a smile, "I know less than you."

Leonard entered the room and asked, "What's going on? Who is that woman?"

"Ada, Lady Grace's nanny." Replied Thomas.

"What did she want? Where's Grace?"

"That little woman left cursing and shouting. She told me to prepare for a duel, then slapped me on the face. Bloody lunatic!"

Leonard tried to follow Ada but Andrew grabbed him by the arm.

"Wait…it's you! You are taking my clothes and my name."

"Yes!"

"What is this new extravaganza?"

"Grace of Scott Winds," Leo replied cold sober "She's pulling all my strings; I'm crazy in love with her. I'm not coming back to the palace."

"Are you insane?" Cried Andrew.

"It's too late…" Leo responded and he disappeared after Ada.

Andrew turned to Thomas rubbing his cheek, and exclaimed furiously, "Bloody jerk! I could be dead in the confusion."

"Ha, ha, ha…fools." Thomas laughed amused.

Twenty six

"I love you without knowing how, or when, or from where,
I love you simply, without problems or pride"
- Pablo Neruda

Grace packed her things in bags and she rode back to Leo; in her way, she saw her nanny walking exhausted on the road.

"What are you doing here?"

"Milady, I'm afraid to confess these horrors, but I love you as my own child. Providence have mercy of us!" The woman said in a crying voice.

"What is it, nana? Speak." Grace approached her.

"Oh, milady, that love of yours is a nothing but a notorious liar, an evil man," she coughed and tried to catch her breath.

"What happened? You're scaring me."

"He went to a tavern, and the Baron confronted him. Andrew denied you. He said he has never met your acquaintance and ran away to the back door as a vulgar thief." The servant broke into tears.

Grace turned pale, "When did that happened?"

"Last night."

"That's impossible!" She exclaimed- "I've been with Andrew every night…and last night…we…" -Grace blushed.

"Oh, my lady, no…no your chastity, if you father finds out…ah," –the old women bent over. Grace jumped from the carriage-"Nanny…"

Ada didn't respond. She was ready to faint. She knew her own head was at risk. Next she prayed, *"Our father in heaven, hallowed be…"*

"Come on, get in the carriage."

"What are you going to do?" Whispered Ada, suffocated.

"Something, I ought to …decipher this damn puzzle, hold on tight!" She said, whipping the horses furiously. Grace would not allow destiny to play her a bad joke.

If Andrew was vicious, and his only intention was to take advantage of her, she was going to tell her fiancé to avenge the insult.

"Why did he deny me? Why?" She tough. Soon, they saw the château, and from a distance, they could see two men arguing on the shore.

Old Age

"Answer me, father. Why not to come with me?"

Leonard and his father were outside. Leo tried to go after Ada, but his father called him.

"Come with me to my palace, you're better now."

"NO. I'm going nowhere, son," he walked towards the water- "My time has come."

"Father come to your senses. You're getting better."

"I seized the crown," added the somber man-"I dethroned my own brother."

"He was not executing!"

"I betrayed God's will."

"He became a tyrant, unloved by the people," Leo ran after the old man.

"My brother became mad…and so did I," Phil stopped and took a good look at his son, and said, "I betrayed you too."

"No…no, father, please."

"Leonard, I'm proud of you… I'm sorry, I did not comfort you when your mother died."

"Please come. The water is cold."

"You know son, I have to admit you turned out to be a great sovereign…against odds!" He laughed, then coughed- "I never was the father you deserved; I only was the father I could be

…You forgive me my boy, god forgives me, I am a sinner…and a drunk…"

Leonard felt the imminent end.

"Uhh"-Phil felt a pain in his abdomen, and cried "I love you…far beyond death," and he took a deep dive into a wave.

"FATHER!"

The old man disappeared into the ocean. Leonard dived into the cold water; a few minutes passed, and he felt terror until he saw Phil's unconscious body floating. He swam towards him, and a huge wave covered them, but he managed to reach the beach. Leo placed the old King on the shore, then checked him, resting his ear on his chest. Philippe was alive. Leo moved the old man's arms, who coughed and splattered sandy ground with crimson blood.

"Father, breathe, breathe!" Next, a familiar voice repeated after him.

"Father?" Grace was looking at him with her pupils dilated as a full moon.

"YES!"

"If that is your father, you have to be…."

"I'm the King. Go to the castle and call for help; my father is dying. GO!" Grace could not do anything but run to the castle, feeling her heart beating as a drum.

 Twenty Seven

King's tomb

Desolated and in complete abandonment, Leonard returned to his palace with his father's body in a hearse. The lifeless body of King Phillipe confirmed Leo's loneliness. Lady Grace denied him an audience. Her father was in shock when he knew the events, and demanded the King not to make public the humiliation. Under the circumstances, her wedding with the Baron was cancelled, and the Lord sent his disloyal daughter to a monastery. "I've never been more offended!" Connery said to his daughter when she boarded a ship to France.

On a different boat, Leo grieved in private. He was sea sick and remained in his cabin with the door locked. His best friend was surprised to see that his majesty returned untouched food and wine all day. Almost at sunset, the servant tried again, "Come on, open the door!" Said Andy, carrying a tray.

"Leave me alone."

"Don't be a child…"

"I don't want to see you, or anybody else!"

Andrew sang, "*My knees are weak; my heart is set, blessed I was with your sweet love. Although briefly, now I know, the happiness that many long.*"

"You don't amuse me," Leo shouted from the other side of the door.

"I brought your medicine, milord." Finally, the lock opened. Sitting on a bench, Leo looked deplorable. He took the bottle and kicked the tray that was still in the hands of his friend.

"The lady is too good for thy!" The servant said angrily.

"If you care for your life, don't show your bloody face again!" Leo yelled, pushing his friend outside the cabin.

Annoyed, Andrew made a sign and sent away the rest of the service-"Don't disturb him."

By Sunday morning, King Phillipe's casket was placed inside the cathedral, at the center of the altar. Leo stood weightless with the other monarchs. A ritual long mass in Latin and a requiem was performed by a monk's choir, the Archbishop, and two priests. Present were the members of the court; nobles and commoners alike got together in an elaborate ceremony to bid farewell to his

Royal Highness. The ritual wasn't long but for Leo, last an eternity, he felt encapsulated.

"I've lost my father and the woman I love the same day"- He knelt during the mass, *"Why love is so painful?"* -He closed his eyes unable to stop a cascade of tears.

Within days official plans were sketched out for a funeral ceremony in a crypt for the fallen king. A mausoleum with a superb tomb with the effigy monument of King Philippe made of granite. A ceremony was scheduled to place the body in St. Matthews's chapel inside the Cathedral, where relatives and former kings and queens were also buried. Gustave and Felicity attended the funeral.

"See, they are mortal!" -Said the wicked woman with shaking hands. "Leonard would die as his ancient father did" - Affirmed the woman covering with a black veil, hiding the purple marks on her neck and face. Signs of his husband's violent temper.

"How do you know?" Gustave growled.

"I always know…." -She said, feeling pain all over her body full of bruises. "You have achieved so much. Make a statement, and give me the crown of Norland next," Felicity whispered in her husband's ear.

Love song

The lady of Scottwinds didn't change her mind. Her confessors advised her that the ultimate solution was a committed life of celibacy in a convent; offered to the service of God as a nun in a Catholic Abbey, fare away from Leo's kingdom. The King back in his palace felt miserable. His love for Grace increased by separation. Powerless to exercise authority in the Abbey, his last resort was to write to the lady.

Beloved Grace, what an impact you have on my life,

Each letter he wrote expressed his deep emotions.

Your memory, gives me a reason to survive and sets me insanely on fire.

He didn't lie to her. Everything was a misunderstanding.

With you, I have experienced an immense affection that I never felt before.

He was completely honest in every letter he wrote.

Constant thoughts mortify me; the conception of how much pleasure we can share, if you allowed this precious love to flourish.

And he didn't receive any reply to his multiple letters.

As immense as whole life is, your absence I breathe. Then something inside me dies, without remedy each night.

There is no domain, no conquest, and no fortune worth having, if I don't have you. You already have my all,

Sitting on his desk, the King was writing his last petition, when Andrew stormed into his chamber and made the announcement he was waiting for, "Milord, there is a lady in the hall, and she demands an audience" -Leo ran like a kid through the corridors. He only had one desire; take her in his arms again and forever. When he arrived at the hall, he yelled with surprise.

"YOU... What are you doing here?"

"To love is to suffer, to avoid suffering
one must not love"
- Woody Allen

Twenty eight

Saint Benedict's Abbey

Novice Grace laid on her side on the cold bed. She had not been able to sleep for days, her mind running uncontrollably. By mornings she would gather enough pride to compose herself and go about her duties in the monastery. Nevertheless, the nights tormented her with the recollection of her love for Leo. She hated to admit that she was foolishly deceived by the adorable monster. Her soul bled full of agony with the idea of living without him. Trying to forget the wicked King was worse than death. Then death had to be the only possible blessing, "If, at least, I would not be carrying his child," she sighed.

"I would find peace in perishing, ending this tormented existence. But pregnant? I do not have the strength to kill myself!"

A pile of unopened letters was sitting on her dresser. She was not going to allow more lies.

Feeling depressed, she took her rosary with the intention of praying, hoping for some peace. "How long can I cover the appearances?" She sat on the edge of the bed- "What if he marries another woman? How can I confront my father again?"

The rosary fell to the floor. "*Oh, God...take me with thy...*"- Her watery eyes closed. Then out of nowhere, she heard a disturbance, the high-pitched noise of metal grinding, and a low but noticeable thud. Grace rose from her bed swiftly; above it, there was the tiniest nook. It would be almost an offense to have called it a window, but through that tiny hole, Grace tried to get a glimpse of the racket going on in the courtyard. She was only able to spot shadows. She made an effort to count them "three"... yes, three shadows. Three sisters running towards the dorms. Grace tried to conceal the events.

"What is all this noise....Unless, no?" -she quickly pushed the thought away. "It cannot be Leonard...maybe bandits."

She didn't know what to do; surely, she had to alert the mother superior. "*Where were her quarters?*" The young nun realized she wasn't familiar enough with the monastery.

"The best is to stay here, until somebody else resolves." But her thoughts were interrupted by a loud banging on the door. Grace faced the door, frozen in fear. She could hear chatter on the other side. The banging persisted; it was obvious some vandals meant to enter the room. The door was giving in… one more bang… Grace shut her eyes tight, and the door swung open violently. Andrew dressed as a nun, finally broke and the old wooden door open. The young novice was standing motionless in the middle of the room.

"Hurry milady, the coast is clear," said Ada, holding hostage an old nun.

"Come on!" Leo didn't hesitate and pulled Grace out of the room. She barely had time to realize what had happened. They headed downstairs towards the main hall of the monastery. Andrew was in the lead, sprinting with ease. They could hear doors opening and shut. Surely someone else had heard the commotion.

In an instant, they made it into the courtyard and outside the gate. In front, a black carriage waited for them, Andrew swung the tiny door open and Leo deposited Grace inside the carriage. With no time wasted, they headed over to lead the horses for a quick getaway. Grace sat in the carriage, still in shock. Leo was trying to catch his breath when she slapped him hard across the face.

"But why?" He yelled.

"HOW DARE YOU!"

"What?"

"Kidnaping me, dressed as a nun...I'm not sure who you are anymore."

He rapidly got rid of the outfit.

"Grace, marry me," his cheeks turned red, and his hair was a mess. "I know you are with child."

"You want the heir; that's what it is, right?"

"Yes…No…I WANT YOU!" He said and kissed her intensely. He disarmed her resistance. Yet, she was doubtful and gazed at him- "You are a notorious deceiver, and I was a fool."

"I lie for you."

"Let me go; I want to stay in the Abbey."

"No, you don't…. You'll be my wife, the Queen of Norland."

"NO... Not, even if you were the last man on Earth," she resisted.

"Ah….ha, ha, ha."

"What's so funny?"

"You can't love any other man; you're mine."

"How pretentious you are!"

"Maybe so, but a spell was cast, and I can't be without you. I need you like the air I breathe," he stared at her honestly, and kissed her passionately.

"Ah!" Ada smiled, relieved.

> *"Whatever the souls are made of,*
> *his and mine are the same."*
> *- Emely Bronte*

Twenty nine

Navigator Starship:
Warrior I-Cosmos 24X-Infinity.

Baylor put on his helmet, fastened his seat belt, and took the shuttle controls. Inside the ship, the smell was synthetic and the temperature low. The bay door opened slowly and revealed a majestic view of darkness and stars,

"OK, here we are. Everybody ready at their post." He opened the circuits and made the ship ready.

"Eagle, prepare for rescue operation, air pressure and oxygen adjusted." Victoria announced.

"Yes, commander!"

A computer added, "Communication channels clear and active."

Victoria noticed, "Time of contact 23 minutes 14 seconds. Preflight checklist completed."

A couple of minutes of silence followed by a feminine computerized voice started the launch count, "Ignition sequence beginning in five, four, three, two ... "

Baylor felt the adrenaline rise to his brain at the moment the shuttle was fired into the vast universe. His stomach contracted like in a roller coaster.

"Oh, God….here we go," he exclaimed crossing the universe.

"Keep course steady, Eagle."

"Roger." He answered with sweaty hands.

"My hands are wet, like in my wedding day" -he noticed amused.

"What did you say, Eagle?"

"I can see her, dressed as a bride."

"Eagle, I need your complete focus in this mission!"

"Yes, commander… Course is steady, Warrior One." And his ship flew easily like a bird in the sky. Floating in the middle of a black frozen ocean, millions of miles away from Earth, like a miracle, like a dream; a warm feeling conquered his heart. The image of his wedding day came to his mind like lightning, *"Grace….my bride….my love, soon we'll be together."*

"By experiencing love, we raise the
conscience to a divine plane. "
- Dalai Lama.

Wedding day

The sonorous cathedral bells toiled throughout the morning with an inviting chant. The crowd was cheering as the chariots arrived. Monarchs of all nations were wearing exotic clothes designed for the royal event. Everybody showed a great pleasure to be part of the wedding of the century. Standing at the altar, looking elegant and handsome, Leo had sweaty hands.

He was next to the priest ready to perform the ceremony. A flood of thoughts overwhelmed the groom. He smiled to Andrew, who asked him cynically, "Nervous?"

"Oh, Lord. You have no idea. I just want to make her happy, that's all."

"She will be," answered his friend.

The royal guard announced the arrival of the bride with trumpets. Leo felt a rush of blood and let out an anxious cough, "I wish the ceremony and festivities were over, and we will be alone." He murmured.

"Easy tiger, the time will come," Andrew hissed in Leo's ear, provoking a smile. The fanfare sound loud and the guests turned to see the bride standing at the entrance of the church, radiating happiness.

A living doll dressed in a fantastic gown gold and satin embroiled with gold trim and pearl brocade. People at the sanctuary murmured by seeing her walking on her father's arm, looking like a spring blossom. She moved with floating feet and the groom was waiting for her with an inviting smile, making her heart pump quickly. It was time to start a new chapter, a new life. She stared at him through the transparent veil thinking he couldn't look more handsome.

Her father stopped at the altar and she made a pray as Leo took her shaking hands.

"Lord, make me his joy and never wrenched him with sorrows."

The ceremony started and the choir sang an Ave Maria directed by the orchestra of St. Michael Chapel. A combination of happiness and excitement overwhelmed the audience. Soon, wedding vows filled the church like sparking butterflies.

I Grace promise…….   I Leonard promise you

To love you……   and honor you….

In sickness and in heath….

All the days of my life…..

Lady Grace, do you take this man?

I do……

King Leonard do you…?

I do……

These rings are symbols of your vowels

With this ring I wed you……

In the name of the Father, the Son....

I PRONOUNCE YOU....

Husband and wife.........

You may kiss the bride!

At the end of the ceremony, the newlyweds greeted the crowd outside the cathedral. The kingdom joined the celebration with hurrahs and songs of love stories. The feast and banquets continued until dawn. For many, it became an unforgettable event. Tales and sonnets were composed in their honor and passed from one generation to another.

Months later, during a scented April afternoon, the queen suffered several hours of labor pains.

Doctors and midwives were helping with the birth to a firstborn boy. A blond baby, charming as his mother, heir of the vigor and strength of his father. By holding his newborn son, Leo sadly realized his heart had been tarnished by pain for many years. He could see clearly, how much resentment he felt against his long- life curse and his father. A few weeks later; the day of the baptism of the little prince, the proud father decided to visit the tomb of King Philippe. After the ceremony, a royal carriage arrived at St. Matthews Chapel. Walking to his father's grave, Leo was carrying his son in his arms.

"The day my father died I was full of rage, I felt betrayed by both of you." Said the King to his wife, "Now Providence has blessed us with a son. I know happiness as never before." He approached the grave and looked at the mausoleum.

"Father, this is my son... Julian...your grandson!" He cleared his throat and held his wife's hand, "This is Lady Grace, Queen of Norland, and the ruler of my heart." He uncovered the baby- "This little lad won my heart the moment I saw him, because it happens that he has a bit of you," He handed the baby to his wife. Next, he kneeled and touched his father's monument, and whispered. "I've lived full of hate and resentment for so long.

I blamed you for my misfortune, my solitude, and your sickness. I was so hard on you. ...and you had nothing but love for me. Forgive me, father," he put his forehead next to his father's granite head. "I wish we could do it over again... do it right!"

He remained kneeled for some moments, his eyes watered, then raised and kissed the statue. The circle of life continued, a new chapter was open. He was married now and started a family.

The Queen, moved by emotion, walked out in silence. The young couple took the chariot back to the castle to proceed with the festivities of the christening of Prince Julian, the new heir. Leonard ordered an inscription in memory of his father. A poem that he wrote himself to honor his memory:

Farewell, oh dear, oh father.
Fate took you away,
One bitter day,
My own blood,
Your face I shall see no more,
I'm afraid some cold nights,
My broken orphan heart,

Won't resist the pain,
To know that no one would love me,
Like you did,
But your light shines inside me,
And it will guide the pad,
Where we finally meet,
Once more.

Thirty

Navigator Starship: Warrior I-Cosmos 24X-Infinity

In a matter of minutes, the shuttle arrived at its destination; the main ship. A giant red nebula of nuclear waste had severely damaged the oxygen systems. Emergency convertors provided oxygen temporarily for more than 2,000 refugees living onboard the starship at risk of perishing. There was no time for mistakes. The operation had to be precise. A small hatch of the shuttle opened, letting the androids out. One by one, they landed on the surface of the ship to start the meticulous repair. Leo was astonished by the harmonious performance of the androids landing slowly and accurately on top on the ship, as a perfect ballet.

"Warrior One to Eagle, over ..." Commander Victoria appeared on a screen.

"Eagle here, the team is landing without a problem. The color of the cloud has changed to purple, over."

"Your perception is correct. The radiation level and temperature are considerably lower. "

"I know, I can read too…" -Leo smiled sarcastically to the screen.

"Keep orbit and channels open." Victoria ordered.

"Yes, Commander."

The team replaced the damaged compartments diligently. Leo got excited to see the robots working in perfect synchrony. "Good job, fellas!"

"Keep the speed steady, Eagle." The robot leader answered with a nasal voice.

"Roger." Leonardo tried to spot Earth, but they were too far away. Not even the Sun was visible anymore. At that moment, he felt an immense desire to be thankful, "Earth...what an extraordinary planet!"

He completed the third orbit, and a gloomy feeling invaded him. He growled, and took a sip from his flask. The ship moved too closed to the mission.

"Everything fine, Eagle? Respond." Asked one of the androids.

"Yes, everything fine," Leo answered and took back the control "Go on… tin can men, don't mind me."

"Are you drinking, Eagle?" His commander inquired, "Where did you..?"

"Where did I get it? I perform tricks, remember. Runs in the family Victoria, now stop the fuss; I'm trying to make a living." He nagged and took another sip of whisky, obviously ignoring his superior.

"You old age, I should have sent somebody else,"

"Too late, time to listen to Mozart," he said, and played his music, feeling lonely, trapped; cold as the frozen black space. Soon, the music captivated him with memories of his past. *"Thanks to God, I lived my life in a rock full of life and nature. Sweeter than nectar and honey."*

"Your music is too laud, Eagle, low your volume," Victoria called his attention again.

"Yes, mam. I'm only bored as a Sea Lion, see…" And he yawned as big as he could, covering the screen.

"And you look like one," the crew noticed and laughter was heard.

"Why not, I'm the walrus. Did I tell you that I met Mozart?"- He said, and took another sip of his flask- "The maestro himself, played for me in my castle, what an honor. Unfortunately, I didn't enjoy his visit as I should."

"Be careful, THE FLASK!" – Shouted the commander, as Leo let his bottle open, "STOP, NOW. You don't care for this mission, Mr. Baylor."

"You're wrong. I deeply care for all of you, Earth creatures" -He answered sarcastically twisting the top of his little container – "There, can you see? It's secure."

"Thank you. Now, can you stay still? There's an emergency, here. "

"Relax, Commander. We got this." Baylor adjust the screen and said – "Did I tell you that I owned more than 135 species of exotic animals at one time?"

"No. We'll hear your medieval stories later."

"No. you won't. I tell you now, before I fell asleep and crash this piece of shit."

Victoria decided to be patient, "Be brief."

"It was after I got married that a collection of fauna covered endless acres in my palace. The menagerie of wild and beautiful beast impressed my visitors; cages with rainforest monkeys from the jungles of Saigon. Tigers from Indonesia, colorful birds from the New Continent. Elephants from India, zebras, and giraffes from Tanzania. Most of the animals were wedding presents from kings and emperors" -Said Leo with emotion, allowing his memory to travel through time.

One spring day during the eighteen century

Immersed in a glorious sight, the King was standing in one of the gardens waiting for the nannies to bring out his son Julian. The grassy knoll covered almost the entire area, and the day was beautiful with a clear sky. Manicured rose bushes, planted by his wife, offered a colorful stone path-way that seemed to go on forever. Finally, he saw the golden-haired boy running towards him.

"Come on, son!" -He looked ecstatic to be alive. The King held Julian and tossed him in the air. The sun shone on their happy faces. He kissed the little infant, and the boy's laughter resonated thru the garden. "Come, we see your animals." -Said the proud father with his child in his arms. Suddenly, a desire filled his heart; he wished they could share the experience with other children.

"This could be a public garden…maybe…an animal garden."

Next, he heard a loud voice.

"What is your resolution? …Your majesty?"

As if summoned, Leonard snapped out from his memories of the early morning in the garden.

He sank back into reality. The men from the Parliament were looking at him, and eventually, the whole room went silent. He soon realized there was an expectation for his answer, and he had no clue as to the subject of discussion.

"Your majesty"-Lord Cummings broke the silence- "What is your resolution?" He repeated.

The room waited for the King to speak. Leo tried to cover his distraction. So, he spoke, improvising his way out of the spotlight.

"I think," He started and touched his lips with his index, "I would like… to… hear, more. More about the matter, before a resolution" -He finished pokerfaced, hoping he had fooled his audience.

"What else is there to discuss?" Yelled an elderly Lord who stood up. "They are taking our resources across the ocean, and we are not seeing a shilling back."

"There is no bustling economy in the new world; there is no way they could come up with enough profit to satisfy YOUR standards!" A young lord retorted.

"What do you mean, gentleman?" The old man replied.

"I shall be clear. I mean… is not enough to satisfy your thirst for gold." There was an uncomfortable silence.

"This is an insult!" The old man blushed, offended. Soon the room broke into a chaos of arguments.

"*They overwhelm me*," Leo thought. Happy to have distracted the attention away from himself. He shrugged, sank back into his chair, and returned to his daydreaming -"*A second child*!" -Yes, Grace was pregnant and due in several months.

Leo couldn't feel happier. The kingdom of Norland had enjoyed relative peace for a long time, agricultural advancement had led to breakthrough technology that, in return, grew the country's finances. Then came an era of wealth and steady richness. The best minds in the land were free to roam the universes of literature, science, and arts. The leaders rose and created a Unified Parliament. An elitist entity of its own, composed of the wealthiest members of society.

Thirty One

The New Parliament

The fresh wind of March blew into the room full of rhetorical men. The clock clank at two hours past noon. The House of Lords continued enclosed, unable to reach an agreement. Midday sun roasted the highlands with its glimmer. They had been talking for hours. Leonard was trying his hardest to be patient. Sir Kane from the Great First Counsel stood up and stated aloud- "The members of the Parliament know, that you are telling not the truth Sir Lambert, and your conduct has dishonored these enclosures." Noise was in the house.

"I will take my oath for it!" Said Sir Kane trying to control the crowd.

Sir Lambert rose and shouted, "On the contrary, Sir Kane, the rumors against your name are bigger than ever; we do not need your oath. Your intentions damage the members of the New Alliance," cried an old man while pointing at his adversary.

"Order!... Order!" shouted Lord Braswell.

The upper parliament was full of the most bizarre men, all with entirely opposite alliances. There were those who remained loyal to the crown, most out of fear.

They thought of Leo as an evil sorcerer. Others supported him out of faith and although they could not settle the mystery of his longevity. It was his long life that allowed their wealthy families to preserve their aristocratic position for generations. They remained loyal as a sign of gratitude. Count Silber's family belonged to that group.

The other side of the opposition took the floor the rest of the afternoon. The new group called; *The Alliance* was innovative and had radical ideas. After thinking it through, his majesty stood up and said:

"There is nothing wrong with being young, and having a vision for the future, write new manifestos…however, we cannot oppress the colonies with these new policies and increasing taxes… is a mistake. I will not risk the peace of the realm. Instead, I want to unify the small surrounding kingdoms, and consolidate a big nation."

The men yelled at each other incoherently. Some about too much power for the crown. Some of the worries for corruption within the allied lands, and others about the need to increase the military in the colonies. Only construction and expansion of the realm enjoyed popular vote.

So, the restless sovereign had no alternative but to insist on continuing the arduous task of rebuilding.

Lord Braswell, the monitor of the room, was calling their attention, "Gentlemen, order....order in the room!"

For years, Leo worked hard on the restoration of the city after a devastating fire destroyed half of the kingdom. Renaissance Palaces; Cathedrals, Opera Houses, Harbors, Ports, and Gardens with extraordinary fountains were built. The King emphasized that building with excellence would preserve the power of the kingdom.

"Lord Braswell, Lord Braswell," Leo bent to him and whispered.

"Yes, milord."

"Close the session. I'm tired. It's late!"

"Yes, your majesty."

Leo couldn't stay longer. The opposition was tying his hands regularly. He spent most of his days in Parliament frustrated and unable to accomplish resolutions.

Lord Braswell closed the session, and the gentlemen left the room one by one, agitated and continuing their discussions outside.

In the end, three shadows remained in the chamber; Lord Charles Norton, Count Lambert, and Sir Kane went out of the room quietly looking for a discreet place to talk. Their faces were somber, and their hearts full of range. One purpose united them, the deep desire to destroy a man and his kingdom.

"There has to be a way to eliminate the tyrant from the face of the Earth!" Affirmed Sir Kane.

"There is a way," said Charles Norton salaciously.

Thirty two

Queen Grace couldn't take her eyes off the field; it was not the flowers that caught her attention or the slope of snow-capped mountains in the distance, but her little boy, who was running amongst the gardens. Julian stumbled face down into the grass. Grace sprung out into the field to him. The prince cried as he embraced his mother.

"There, there you're fine baby," she consoled him, "I'm here now." She thought he was brittle, yet he was not. He had to be immortal. But she was not sure yet…

"There's a lady who's sure,
All that glitters is gold,
And she's buying a stairway to Heaven."
- Led Zeppelin.

Grace kept it secret. A few days before her wedding, she returned to her father's home. She was vigorously looking for an old trunk. Property of her great-grandfather. The same man that manipulated old King Philippe to meet the Alchemist.

Prisoner of immense desire, she knew, she had to act quickly, so she took all the wizards' books and tools from a secret trunk, property of her ancestors. With great determination; she penetrated the deepest forest, after riding for miles, she finally found a famous stone cabin.

An old dirty place with a strong odor of dead. She stepped inside; the site was unoccupied. The young bride rested on the floor, her basket full of books and potions she carried from her ancestor's home. Her hands were red, and her load was heavy, but her heart was settled. Grace was determined to share Leonard's curse, a life of a thousand years. Her eyes scanned the place; she noticed jars, animal furs, and spider webs occupying every inch of the racks inside the cabin. She didn't hesitate and called for help.

"Hello!" Her voice resonated in the forest. The young maiden had accepted Leo as her life companion, soon, her marriage would take place in the Cathedral, she was never more confident of her decision, yet her hands were shaking. Suddenly, a creepy voice greeted her.

"Welcome milady, I've been waiting for you." Said a dreadful woman, dressed in black. Her face was covered with a black veil, and the shadows disguised her robust male features. Grace's heart was pumping hard. She fixed her attention on the old woman and, with a trembled voice, said, "I need a potion."

Ophelia approached her and took the basket. She looked at it and the content of the books and jars, "A potion, milady?...Are you sure?"

Grace nodded.

The witch took a cauldron and filled it with herbs. The future queen sat on a trunk. She wanted to empty her mind. What if the potion would kill her? What if they blame Leonard? He wasn't aware of her choice. She talked to no one about meeting the witch. The young bride took deep breaths and waited patiently for the witch to finish her enchantment. Ophelia finally spoke, "With this beverage, you'll live a long life as your beloved husband and every child you conceive."

Grace looked at her with dread, a second of doubts crossed her mind, and a ton of apprehension sank her on the grown, she felt her blood frozen, but her feelings for Leo whispered in her heart and gave her courage. The sorcerer took Grace's hand and said, "Drink, my child."

The future queen closed her eyes, "This is my deepest desire. So be it!" And she drank to the last drop -while a flock of birds took flight, shaking the leaves at the center of the woods.

I believe in dragons; I've seen them in my nightmares…

A little boat went afloat with ease; Queen, and Prince, sat in it passively, a most unusual thing for Julian, who was an active boy.

Leo could see them floating away into the distance.

Suddenly, the skies turned dark, as angry clouds formed above them. The young father was to fare from them. He had a bad omen. As if summoned by his thoughts, an enormous wave the height of a wall appeared from the horizon. The Alchemist, his all-time enemy, was in the boat with his family. How was that possible? The King ran to the shore, "Look out!" -Leo cried horrified, but no sound escaped from his mouth. His wife and child were captives now.

"NOO!…" Leo's deaf screams echoed only in his mind. The enormous wave reached the boat and stuck it. Engulfing them in dark waters, leaving nothing in its path. The grey waters, suddenly changed color; axes, shields, spears, and swords were floating on an infinite crimson ocean and also hundreds of dead soldiers….

"The destiny of a man is written in his own soul"
- Herodotus

Grace sat up-right next to him.

"Milord, wake up, wake up," she cried, concerned, as she held him. Leonard looked at her with relief.

"Grace, love…"

"You were shouting."

"A dreadful nightmare," he replied. There were drops of sweet on his forehead.

Grace was concerned. The recurring dreams were a constant sign of his agitated spirit.

"Here, drink some water."

"I'm fine."

"Maybe you should consult your advisors." She said with determination, "some dreams contain revelations and are prophetic."

"I don't know… usually, dreams don't mean anything."

"For some people…but, you… you are the King!"

"Let's go back to sleep."

"Leonard, I insist!"

He took a deep breath, and said, "If it gives you comfort, I'll see Cahill tomorrow. Sleep now," he answered and covered her with blankets. He fluffed his pillow and turned his back. He wondered if the nightmares were a sign of war. A message which foreshadowed the end of his kingdom.

Thirty three

Fortune Teller

Dr. Michael Cargill, the astrologist, was his favorite advisor.

The 65-year-old man, loyal to the crown, lived in the western tower of the palace, located atop cliff. The next morning his majesty decided to pay Cargill a visit. While climbing the spiral staircase made of marble stones, the fresh memory of his previous dream rolled over him, making him very uncomfortable with the idea of listening to nothing but bad news. Cargill never sugar-coated his predictions. He was visionary and crude -a skillful interpreter of the signs of the sky.

As soon as Leo opened the door, an aroma of incense and burning leaves invaded his senses.

"I was wondering when you'd finally have the courage to see me, milord." Said a voice from behind a large bookcase. Not many got away with taking to the King disrespectfully, but the old man saw right through Leo's heart and was able to read him like a book.

"I've been having these, recurring nightmares."

"I know; I'm glad you're paying attention." He answered, scratching his white beard.

"I can't ignore them any longer."

"We all shall look for answers," Michael replied, emerging from behind a bookcase. Candles illuminated the room with amber light, giving the old's man face a sumptuous look. He was of average height and wore dark olive robes with a touch of purple and gold, which were entirely too big for him.

On his head rested a rounded lavender turban. His face was determined and calm. He spoke with concern- "Your majesty, there is no good news. I am afraid." He looked at Leo with flashy eyes- "I've been studying the sky for months. There is no doubt. It is Neptune…"

"What's happening?"

"The new position of the planet would bring imminent changes to Earth" -Dr. Cahill showed him charts and continued. "Look at this chart, the prevalent order, the present law ….will succumb." -He said, resting his hands on his stomach.

Leo's knees went weak. He took a seat next to the astrologist.

"Michael, please explain yourself."

"It's simple. The world is changing, milord."

"What exactly are you saying? Is the kingdom under danger?"

"All crowns in the Continent are in danger. War storms shall rage, and oceans of blood would roar…" Michael paused and stared at him through his half-moon spectacles, "Neptune is the seventh house announcing large changes. Revolts, wars, revolutions will happen. Transitions no one can stop. The ancient shall die."

"Do you mean?"

"What I mean is…some monarchies will see the end of their times." The Astrologist pointed his finger at the maps and charts, walked around the room and nodded his head, then bent towards Leo and said, "Your kingdom…. won't be the exception."

Leon felt a ton under his shoulder and asked, "I need to know who's behind this?"

"I'm afraid, many and no one." The wizard stroked his beard with his hand.

"What?"

"Rebels will rule most of the lands." Suddenly he got louder- "Waves…I should say…rivers of blood will flow for years until the revolution would be accomplished."

"Army rebellions?"

"Precisely!"

"Where?"

"Everywhere, milord."

"The funny thing is that I can feel it too." Leo got pale. He wished his advisor was mistaken, but he was not surprised by the prediction. He was aware of the age of a new order. However, with rebellion comes war, and he feared for his kingdom, but most of all, for his family.

"There is another issue."

"Speak…"

"The Alchemist, my enemy from the past. Is he still alive?

Michael Cahill tossed some runes on the table, and stared at them for a moment, then answered somberly.

"Yes, milord. He is."

Leo frozen, he expected a different reply after so many years.

"Where… where is he now? Will we meet again?"

"I do not know!" He moaned and tilted his head, then threw the stones once more. The rune flew on the air, and this time the magician collected them in his pocket after the read. He looked disturbed. His face blushed. "Milord…" he cleared his throat and continued, "there will be an encounter, two actually."

"What do you mean?"

"The first encounter will be violent and will happen shortly."

"And?"

"The second," the wizard hesitated.

"Yes?" Leo asked, thrilled.

"The second will be deadly; only one of you will prevail…"Cargill stared at the King, "I'm afraid it won't be you."

"We'll see," Leo said pail and stood up next to his friend. "What's your advice?" He was pleading for good news. This time the wizard stared at King's pupils. His expression was serious, and his voice resounded in the walls, "You must choose for the safety of the royal family before anything else!"

Leo agreed and left the room, startled.

Thirty Four

Lewis Sylberman

"**M**otion in order!" Announced Lord Braswell.

The assembly was ready to continue with the proposed edict to increase the taxation of the colonies.

"I ask permission to take the floor," said Norton. Mysterious secrecy was handled by the trio inside the House to increase dissatisfaction for the ruler. The King suspected a traitor. As Norton gave his argument for the bill, Leo bent discreetly over Count Silber's shoulder and asked him to follow Norton's movements.

"Yes, milord." Sir Lewis Sylberman babbled not to raise suspicion in the House. The old man was considered a loyal subject and a personal friend to Leo. For generations, the Sylberman House proved their allegiance and total loyalty to his majesty.

The discussion in the House of Lords was endless. There was an irrefutable division among them, and no progress was accomplished on any issue. The King, frustrated, had no option but to suspend the Parliament for two weeks. Once he was outside and ready to take his golden carriage, Sylberman approached him.

"I'll follow Norton, but I also suspect of Sir Kane, milord,"

"Investigate both and any of his associates...and keep me inform, Lewis." Leo said and jumped into his carriage.

"By all means, your majesty." The Lord closed the door and made a little tap for the driver to start the trip. The King felt at ease; by closing the Parliament, he gave the opportunity to cool off tempers and dissolve hatred. He'd lived too long to know treason was a natural process, and there was nothing like time to cure wounds inflicted by wild emotions. With his aging one year, every 12, Leo looked in his late thirties. Thirty-six virtual years had made his majesty tired of the crown, as well as the fashion. The baroque style was popular in Italy and spread around the western world by the Grand Tour of the European Gentlemen.

For his majesty, everybody in the Parliament looked like a bunch of Opera dancers with short tight trousers and delicate shoes; make-up on their faces, and silk dresses.

Inside the carriage, he felt his feet burning, apparently his shoes were too tight, and his toes swollen.

"I'm so sick of these long wigs and cosmetics on my face. How we ended wearing this bloody rubbish!" He commented to the chief of his guard while removing his shoes and cleaning off his face with a handkerchief. He took advantage of being out of side, and noticed with sorrow, he was already losing hair when he flew his wig next to his companion.

"You must be most amused by my misery!"

"No, milord." His guard looked at him with empathy and remained silent. Dogs barked and the floated stopped abruptly, making the passengers lose their balance.

"Hey!" Leo tapped the top of the carriage.

"Forgive me, your majesty; dogs crossed the road!" Shouted the driver. Leo took a look through the window and saw a couple of drunks entering a tavern. He couldn't stop staring at them, and for some inexplicable reason, he felt a chill down his spine; next, he looked up to the sky and noticed dark clouds formed and lightning followed by the roar of thunder.

"Hard times are coming, Morgan."

"We shall stretch our fortune, milord," commented the man next to him. Leonard tried to control a chocking hunch and yelled, "TO THE PALACE!" While the horses whinnied at the crack of a whip and the car sped away.

Affiliation

After a long walk under the rain, Lester Miller pushed the tavern door. With a strong lunge, the door gave in with a chill. Everyone inside stirred.

The robust man hung his wet coat by the entrance and brushed off the rain from his body and long hair. Next, he motioned a bottle towards the barman. Slowly, he approached a large table on the far side of the tavern, right in the middle overlooking everything. In it sat say the elitist customers of the tavern and several other known goons. Lester walked towards them, showing his bottle up to his head. They weren't too fond of him; he was an outcast of ill reputation, capable of anything for some attention and few shillings. However, they would not refuse an invitation to drink another man's alcohol.

"Hello, friend!" One of the fellows stood, Miller received a firm embrace.

"Wocher doing?

"I'm here," he opened the bottle and stared at his audience, "looking for business."

"Ah…you have a job in hand!"

"Perhaps…are you interested?" Asked Lester Miller, showing teeth and serving scotch in little glasses.

"Depends on the pay," one drifter noticed.

"My customer is wealthy…" Miller replied, lowering his voice- "a Lord in need… of a clean job and a mob with determination."

"That's us, we're on," the scumbags laughed.

A mysterious man entered the pub, dressed in black, wearing a big coat and large hat, totally cliché. He noticed Miller and sat next to him to explain the mission. The group listened attentively and felt like the universe was conspiring with them.

"If you accomplished the task, your reward will be generous."

"Who is the brains of this job? We need to know," Miller asked.

"You need to know nothing! You're hired to act, not to know."

"Then, tell us… who we have to kill?"

There were some seconds of silence, then the stranger took a sip of his glass and said, "The bloody Queen…"

They laughed once more.

"She's a dead as a door nail; you count on us!" Answered Miller.

They toasted and cracked up as the thunderstorm roared.

Thirty Five

Opulent Melody

While posing for hours for his favorite portraitist, Leo was sweating copiously. His throat was dry, and his hand was reaching for a drink from a golden cup.

"Don't move, milord!" Yelled the artist. A gigantic portrait of the King was to be displayed in the Parliament, but posing for the portrait was a pain. His lower back was killing him. The tension and stress of the recent months were reflected in his muscles; he needed to change posture. His only indulgence at the moment was the sweet music in the chamber.

"Magnificent composition, Maestro!" The King smiled at the young composer, who was playing the piano, accompanied by a violin and a cello.

"Your majesty, please…don't move," A frustrated complaint came from behind the canvas.

"A man can die but- once!" Leo answered the artist and laughed.

"Oh…Milord…the portrait would be magnificent."

Leo didn't care much; the painting wasn't his idea but a suggestion of his advisor, Lord Sylberman. The old man insisted on the importance of showing who the ruler of the Parliament was. That morning, Leo was clothed in a gold embroidered rococo gown which consisted of an exuberant coat, a velvet waistcoat, and breeches, all in red, topped with a long powdered wig and a huge black hat with feathers.

For the portrait, on his right hand was a golden staff adorned with gems. Next to him was Rex, his favorite dog. A white and black English Shepherd that loved his master deeply.

After hours of posing for the portrait, his mind was finally distracted by the richness of the melody. Sweet music that resounded in the palace. "Bravo!" -Shouted Leo- "What's the name of the piece Maestro?"

Young Mozart was visiting the realm, indulging the court with his unique talent. Lewis Sylberman interrupted the scene entering with urgency the chamber, followed by the King's guard.

Leo was relieved to see him. He was anxious for news.

"Lewis!...Always a pleasure to see you," He made a sign for him to step closer.

Once next to the King, he spoke softly.

"We have news, your majesty."

"I'm listening,"

"Your suspicions are correct. My spies discovered evidence against Norton."

"How bad?"

"Enough to accuse him of treason."

"Who else is with Norton?"

"Lambert and Kane," Lewis sighed.

Leo took another sip of his cup and spoke firmly.

"Arrest and execute Norton."

"Yes, milord."

"To Sir Lambert…offer the greedy man a generous amount of gold and some land in the north. Make sure, he understands; we have enough evidence to take him to the gallows. "

Sylberman managed to control his emotions.

A chilled silence was produced.

Lewis was afraid to talk, yet he bowed, "Milord," inquired softly "And Sir Kane?"

Kane and Sylberman were related, and Leonard knew both families well. Leo stared at Sylberman, then spoke freely, "Kane has great influence in the parliament. Simply make sure he received the message that I've been generous for generations with his family, and I appreciate his valuable experience and presence in the House."

"I understand, milord."

Leo held his friend by the arm, "also, remind him that the tower is large and has enough room for traitors and every member of their families."

The earl managed to control the frenetic desire to slap Leonard's face. *"How long has the kingdom put up with thee?"* Sylberman thought.

"So it will be done, your Majesty," Lewis nodded, and with rapid steps, went to the door.

"Lewis….my friend." Leonard called him. He froze and turned back nervously.

"Don't forget tonight we're celebrating Maestro Mozart's visit."

Mozart waved him with a handkerchief joyfully.

"Certainly, there is no other talk in the palace." The Lord noted, pretending joy.

Magic Flutes of Champaign,
Silver Trays with Canapes,
Raise our spirit tonight,
We shall dance,
Until the sunrise.

The orchestra could be heard thru several rooms in the palace. The royal couple and court were practicing the *Minuet*; a new dance with delicate baroque steps and spatial pattern marking for a flirtatious interlude. Queen Grace looked radiant in a French-style green and gold dress with large hips, making her three-month pregnancy inconspicuous. The couple was skillful in the dances, and their spirits were rising by sparkling wine. One of the invitees, the French ambassador, asked for a private audience with Their Majesties during the party.

In high spirit, Leo led the diplomat to one of the rooms to talk in private. "Are you having a good time, Monsieur?" Leo asked him, trying to catch his breath after dancing almost all night.

"Great party, your majesty," answered the refined man with a French accent.

"Wonderful present this sparkling wine!"

"Thank you, milord," he cleared the throat, "From the region of Champaign."

"Ah, splendid...We need more!" Leo laughed.

"Avec Plaisir. Excusez-moi if I am not following protocol and I interrupted the ball."

"We're busy men, Ambassador," the king offered him a seat, "I understand you have a message from your sovereign."

"Oui, milord. The King of France is requesting the pleasure of your company for the celebration of the wedding of his son, Prince Louis." The man delivered a small envelope.

"Une mariage royal, c'est un notice formidable… magnifique!"

"When is the wedding?" Asked Grace while opening the envelope.

"Mai 16,"

"Less than a month!" She covered her mouth.

"Vive l'amour!"

Leo held Grace and started kissing her, "Bien sûr monsieur, nous attendre. Merci mon amie," he opened the room's door, and shook hands with the emissary, "Congratulation to his royal highness! Enjoy the rest of the party." He said and took his wife's hand to return to the main room.

The French Ambassador left the palace pleased with the meeting with the legendary King of Norland, as he wasn't sure what to expect. The regal couple was famous on the Continent. Some fear them; others admire them as jet set superstars. The fame that Leo and Grace didn't take seriously but made efforts to be closer to their loyal subjects. They attended operas, theatres, and plays giving the opportunity to everybody to make their acquaintances. The young queen's beauty became legendary. Poets, musicians, and writers were inspired by her elegance and charisma.

Opulence in the renaissance architecture in Norland was overwhelming. Gorgeous symmetrical facades, marvelous arches; fantastic gold ceilings, manicured gardens, and river walks with fabulous statues dominate the scenario. Adorning the kingdom with incomparable grandiosity and splendor. However, on the far sides of the cities, forgotten communities were not blessed. There were villages scarce of resources, and poverty was the only melody they knew. Most of the people died young.

Malnutrition and unhealthy living conditions were common. Some desperate citizens took the option of selling themselves or their children to the slave trade to avoid starvation.

 Thirty Six

Ravenous

Thomas Miller arrived home from a long day of work at the blacksmiths, his decaying wood home laid in a back alley. The rain had flooded it, and it was surrounded by mud. Miller maneuvered to walk through the puddles with disgust on his face, and carefully opened the creaky front door. He entered his house and proceeded to take off his dirty boots.

Immediately came the deafening screams of the baby girl in the kitchen, the young father was already frustrated.

"Shut that kid up already," he yelled.

"She's hungry," his wife replied. "You haven't brought any food."

She retorted. Miller pulled a big sack from the door; his wife shone for a minute with excitement, from the sac he withdrew, a massive jar of mead, a foul carcass, and potatoes. His wife's glow disappeared. She stared blankly at the meal she was supposed to cook and feed to a husband and three starving children.

"Well, get a cooking woman," he yelled at her "and fetch me a flask. Bloody wife!" He added with contempt. A little girl, dressed in rags, hurried to give him a jar from one of the dusty cabinets.

"Do you really think I'll drink out of this shit?" He violently grabbed the jug and tossed it to the floor; the thick glass shattered against it.

"Clean up the mess," he ordered shamelessly. He grabbed the bottle of mead and exited the home, this time forgetting about the puddles. He spat on the floor cursing his existence and then continued his way towards the tavern. He murmured to himself, "You're dead wench Queen…dead and buried!"

"Poverty is the worst form of violence."
- Mahatma Gandhi

Thirty seven

A Royal Weeding

"**P**eek-a-boo!"

Little Prince Julian giggled uncontrollably, and Andrew could not find a better way to spend time than playing with the baby heir. The contagious laugh of the little creature gave him a joy he hadn't felt in a long time. Sitting in the middle of a lavish room painted light blue and gold. The Baby was running around an innumerable amount of toys. Andrew hid his big blue eyes behind his hands again.

"Where's the baby?... Where's the baby prince?"

Grace entered the room, and behind her a convoy of about a dozen servants carrying various types of fabrics. The maids slammed them on a table, exhausted.

"I see you're going to attend the wedding, after all!" Andrew observed.

"I want to go. My husband needs a distraction from the Parliament, this little trip will make him good." She said examining the different types of fabric.

"Leonard is too extravagant, why is he hiding the trip from the court? It's absurd."

"No, absurd and extravagant is the French fashion, Avant-garde." She claimed, choosing fabrics.

"How many gowns do you need?" Andrew inquired.

"I don't know. Soon, I will be due. I need something that will fit." She answered softly. She made a long pause, and the tender smile disappeared from her face. "I'm not sure if I'm making a fair impression on the Court."

"Oh, milady. Of course, you do. You're beyond fair. They adore you!"

"No, they don't. They pretend I can feel it"-She was concerned- "I fear the future, Andrew," She grabbed her friend's hand.

"You don't have to worry, milady. The safety of the throne is ensured" -He added with passion holding the baby, "One day, Prince Julian will rule these lands, and he will be a great sovereign."

Grace smiled at Andrew and exhaled a tenuous sigh. Her expressions were so transparent that she could not hide the worry in her eyes.

"There's something else, isn't it?" He asked.

"We paid a visit to the sage."

Andrew rolled his eyes, although, he tolerated the ancient tradition; he always thought of it as gibberish, "Don't let them mortify yourself, and fill your head with court gossip."

"No, Andrew, it's more than banal rumors. Dr. Cargill predicted Mercury would bring a new child, blessed with balance and power. Equilibrium will be the spirit of the child, who will lead several nations to a new Kingdom of peace and prosperity."

Andrew took her hands into his. The Queen continued, "Michael said our destiny is to protect this unborn leader until the last minute of our life. Andrew, I just don't know how much I can take."

"Oh, milady," he grinned, "God will bless the King and his successors. Have faith!"

Last days of a kingdom...

The tension in the parliament was stronger than ever. The Royal Guard arrested the famous traitor and put the King's opposition on fire. A large group gathered to discuss the recent events: "Sir Charles Norton, a traitor?" Asked Sir Henry, standing in one of the halls of the Parliament.

"Impossible, the King has been misinformed!" Answered Sir Starr.

"Sir Norton has been accused of being the brains of a conspiracy."

"How can you conceive such a notion?" Asked Henry.

"What a scandal!" Claimed Lord Hobson.

"He was discovered after using the same Modus Operandi. His actions evident like a knitted pattern."

"This would send him directly to the guillotine." Remarked Lord Starr. Commotion was inside the building. Everybody was lauded and distracted. All groups had collided, forcing their ideas and agendas through each other, trying to take out one another. It was chaos. The King saw no strategy or method to tame the effervescent crowd. There was no way to suppress the facts either.

Intense back pain was torturing Leo once more, and with it came a sense of enlightenment. Within a second, he decided, he'd no longer put up with the madness. As if the room was completely empty, he descended the throne and left quickly.

The members of parliament, immersed in the discussion, hardly noticed his absence. Leo kept walking out the front gates, and towards the village, he quickly snatched a cape to conceal himself; he did not want to be disturbed.

"I'm not standing in the middle of Armageddon," said to his guards, who were running after him. They saw him take off his wig and throw his jacket in the air.

"I'm alright, I only need some fresh air!" instructed the guards who allowed him to disappear into the city. Waking fast, he was immersed in reflections; his blood was boiling with anger. He was never an absolutist, or a lenient King, but there was always a percentage of the population who didn't trust him. They died, and he survived, and then a whole new generation of haters was born. Leo had zoned out through the village alleyways and suddenly found himself lost. Everything was covered in dense fog, so the alley next to his eyes was completely new. He tried to find his way back when he heard sweet singing. As if coming from a dream.

He took a few steps toward the figure who was producing the delicate hymn. It was a woman, a beggar. The King took a look at the lady, who was weak and malnourished, clothed in dirty rags. He looked at her carefully; her voice was exquisite, able to calm any soul with an angel's tone. By getting close to her, he realized the woman was blind, but there was no sign of pain in her face. On the contrary, her face lit up to a state of ecstasy.

The hymn was in Latin, and he was familiar with it.

"Pie Jesu (Lord Have Mercy)

Agnus Dei (Lamb of God)

Agnus Dei (Lamb of God)

Qui tollils peccata mundi (You who take away the sins of the world)

Dona eis requiem (Grant them peace)"

Like awakening from a dream, the King looked around and saw a multitude of beggars; some sick, others in a terminal state.

At that moment, he realized that he was in the slums of the city. He took a few coins from his bag and offered them alms. The beggars approached and touched him.

They recognized him by his refined clothes.

"It's the King!" They shouted.

"Majesty, your majesty." They revered him.

He turned back to the signing woman, approached her, and put a coin in her hand. The angel smiled, as she felt the coin. Tenderly she muttered, "God bless you, milord."

Leo was moved to tears. He hadn't seen a face so serene, and peaceful in years. "How?" he whispered "Your face and…"

"I beg your pardon, milord." She answered moving her head towards his voice.

"No, it's me that begs your pardon, milady. Come with me! To my palace, I'm the King."

"I can't." She nodded her head.

"Why not? I'll take care of you."

"And who would take care of them, milord?"

Leo was shocked. He stared at the people who looked at him with awe. He was not aware of the existence of that spot.

"How can I help?" He asked the lady.

"Go back to your palace; there's always a way to ease the misery in the world."

He took her hands and made a petition, "Please… sing…. For me, for my soul."

With high emotion, she began her song.

"Pie Jesu (Lord Have Mercy)

Agnus Dei (Lamb of God)

The melody resounded in the alley as he ran back, and when he turned on a corner, another beggar was waiting for him in the middle of the street, an old man with a grotesque appearance.

"You're not safe!" The lunatic stared at him with dark eyes.

"I… I'm looking for the palace, where's the palace?" He asked puzzled.

"FIND A WAY…FIND A WAY!" The man shouted absent-mindedly, annoying Leo. He raised his arms and cried, "RUN…RUN… BEFORE IT'S TOO LATE, OR THE QUEEN, YOUR LADY WILL PERISH!"

Leo ran to what seemed the main street. With a short breath, finally made it where his guards looked at him with surprise. He jumped into his carriage, feeling his pounding heart, and shouted, "Take me out of here, at once!"

Upon hearing the sound of the horses, he felt the urgency to hold Grace and his son in his arms.

"The saddest thing about betrayal
Is that it never comes from your enemies."
- Anonymous

Thirty eight

The Pain I cause

Grace and Leonard got the distraction and relaxation they were looking for, although, the return home was unusually long.

"I'm happy to be home, what an exuberant celebration!" Said Leo while the carriage entered the city.

"There were no qualms regarding stylish and opulence," said Grace opening her fan.

"Perhaps, but our wedding was better," he remarked, smiling.

"Are you jealous?"

"Me? They should be jealous of us!" He said, embracing his wife.

The French King conquered his guest with luxury and extravagance, but there was a certain air of irritation in his kingdom. The French subjects didn't look so fortunate. Pain and poverty were evident in every face and every corner of the nation. When the carriage crossed the walls of the palace, Leo kissed his queen's hand.

"Welcome home, darling!"

The sun was setting, painting the sky orange. Grace, delighted to be back, opened the window of the carriage for a breath of fresh air. Soon a horrific scene was displayed before their eyes. The heads of Miller and his family, including two children, hung from the tower with a sign that read "*TRAITORS.*"

"NO!" Grace covered her eyes and cried with horror.

"What the hell…? STOP!" He cried, and stepped out. After, he examined the remains, they went home to ask for an explanation.

"Since when we execute children and women?" Leo asked Andrew.

"The rebels attacked the Queen's cartridge and forced it into the river. They didn't know you were out of the Kingdom."

"Unbelievable!"

"They were traitors, milord…They killed Grace's aunt and two of her maids…The women drowned in cold water!"

"Call Lord Sylberman," Leo ordered and looked for his wife. He was sure the primary objective was to agitate the crowds against him. Grace was drinking tea when her husband gave her the news.

"Do you mean…?"

 "Yes, your aunt, Irene, and her maids, all drowned."

Grace's eyes watered, "Oh, my poor aunt! Why…. was this an attack against me?"

"Of course not. This was an accident."

"Don't lie to me, Leonard. I know things are getting rough." She said placing her son in his cradle.

"Please, go to bed and try to rest. We'll talk tomorrow."

"I can't sleep, not like this."

"Do it for the baby, you're with child."

"Oh, my poor children…what will become of them?"

He stared at her, "Rest…now…please, Grace. Help me."

"Only if you stay with me," -she answered sadly- "I'm afraid, I'm so afraid of the future."

"Don't be. Come…you have to be tired."

"I'm exhausted." Grace finally laid by his side. Leo was puzzled and couldn't pretend to be asleep. His head was pounding, and his stomach was growling. He got up from bed carefully, trying not to disturb his wife. When descending the stone stairs to the kitchen, he heard steps approaching him.

His butler, a wimpy man by the name of Raymond, moved toward him nervously"

"Your majesty!" He said almost out of breath-"There are unexpected visits in the main hall."

"Right now? What time is it?"

"It's ten o'clock, milord."

"Dismiss them. I don't want to be disturbed."

"I'm afraid I can't, your majesty."

"Why?"

The servant saw him scared. Loud shouting could be heard from the floor below. Leo hurried toward the room, leaving Raymond panting heavily.

"What's your affair here?" Asked the King, wiping his face.

Gustave of Normandia was drunk and in a deplorable state. His clothes were dirty and, his face pale.

"I came to claim your soul!"

Leonard made a sign to the servants to take Gustave from his sight.

"I AM NOT GOING ANYWHERE!" The big man broke free from the guard.

"Gustave, you picked a bad day. I don't have time for you…"

"The immortal tyrant doesn't have….. TIME."

"It's you the one called tyrant among his own people."

"Do you know why?" Gustave sat on a table arranging his robe.

"You've abused your subjects. They live in misery and darkness.

"Look who's talking?" Gustave said, scratching his white beard with a knife. "If my subjects are abused is because the miserable deserve no compassion," he said, in low voice, "They worship villains like you and me." He laughed.

"You're so cynical. You killed Queen Felicity, your own wife.

"True," he said, with no remorse- "The wicked bitch begged me to shut her up."

"I don't believe you, and you are not my affair, so leave my presence at once!"

"I am not to be judged by you … immortal wizard,"

"Leave, savage MURDERER!"

"Yes, I am a murderer…..But you… how far are you willing to go? How stupid do you think we all are?"

Leonard turned himself and walked out of the room, when he heard Gustave shouting.

"Fight me, or I'll kill this man!"

"That soldier is your own guard." Leo noticed.

"This man is nothing; he is worthless…I can take his life if it pleases me."

"You know no boundaries, lunatic..." Leo took a sword from his guards, "En Garde!"

The two men began to fight. Andrew made a signal to the guards to defend his master, but Leo shook his head and raised his hand, preventing anyone from being involved. They fought vigorously, as they were skillful with swords. They went from one room to another, scratching furniture, curtains, and walls, struggling with uncontrollable anger. Gustave was furious, breaking everything he could, making Leonard extremely angry. Leonard injured Gustave's arm revealing a bleeding cut. Suddenly, Gustave agilely stopped in front of a vast, expensive porcelain vase, an adornment to the room.

"Ohh, No…Gustave…that's from the Ming Dynasty," Leo warned him. Gustave's eyes were on fire, "WAS from the Ming Dynasty." And he knocked the vase to the floor breaking it into pieces.

"You see what you made me do? I'm also broken."

"You're more than broken, evil man."

"Put me back together. Make me the man I used to be. I'll pledge alliance to you!" He shouted with watery eyes.

"IT'S TOO LATE FOR YOU!" Leo shouted and rapidly removed the sword from Gustave's hand, but Gustave had a small pistol in his pocket and fired it, injuring Leo.

The King of Norland bent took a knife hidden on his belt and launched it into Gustave's heart opening it with an explosion of blood. Gustave fell, then laughed and murmured.

"You were the only one who could stop me… send me to hell," He got pale, and with panic, he cried, "They're there….can you see them?….Every single one." He pointed towards a wall.

"Who?" Leo turned his back and saw no one.

"They're waiting for me with blood is in their faces," with strength Gustave took the knife out of his chest and cried- "All those fools. YES!...

I killed YOU ALL… and I'll do it again if I could."

Leo felt dizzy as dense energy covered the room. Was it possible that the victims of Gustave were waiting for his death? He dismissed the thought and saw how the mad man had lost his consciousness.

"Deliver the King to his men," he ordered to Andrew, "And make sure the mess gets clean."

"Yes, milord." Answered the servant, who watched his friend exit the room quickly.

 Thirty nine

"If I am what I have, and if I lose what I have,
Who am I, then?"
- Erich Fromm

Sitting in his favorite hiding spot, a big room with an enormous chimney. Leo groaned in pain as he opened his skin with a knife to take the rest of the bullet in his chest. He poured Scotch inside his wound. The fire illuminated the room with an orange light that concealed his watery eyes. *"Is it possible that I'm becoming Gustave?"* He murmured- *"Am I becoming what I despise most*? He drank a sip of whiskey watering his bitter throat.

"They hate me…and I fear their disloyalty," He thought and touched his forehead with his glass. A lifetime devoted to serving his subjects, in return, he was labeled as a tyrant. An insane, cruel man.

"Ungrateful, disloyal bastards!" He threw his empty glass into the fire. The love and respect of his subjects would be the natural result of his devotion, but life is full of surprises and disappointments. He heard the door open, someone approach him.

"Not now, Andrew!"

But his friend ignored him as usual.

"King Gustave is dead." said relieved, "His men picked up the corpse."

"The soldiers witnessed the scene. They know it was not my will to kill him. The last thing we need is a war with Normandia."

"Oh, no! They expressed resignation." Andrew informed and carried water and bandages.

"Tell me one thing."

"Milord?"

"If I am not the King, who I am?"

"You are and always will be the King,"

"How can I rule my people if they don't trust me? They condemn every act. Maybe I'm becoming a Gustave."

"Madness! He was insane, wicked. Your people love you, they're loyal subjects. You're at the top of the world."

"The greater my power is, the deepest my agony grows."

"Nonsense."

"No, Andrew, things change, we all change."

"But…"

"Life is a constant challenge. A challenge to fight resistance; move forward and change. Either to fly or to fall. Nothing remains static in this world."

"Love, loyalty, friendship doesn't change, milord." Andrew tied his bandages.

"Ah, not so tied." He claimed and stared at his friend, "I am not a coward; I don't run away from circumstances. But let me tell you something of great importance."

"Yes, milord." Andrew stared at him.

"I would never risk the safety of my people or the welfare of my family."

"The Crown is safe. The world is at your command." Recited the servant with passion.

Leonard rested a hand on Andrew's shoulder and smiled- "Indeed my friend, can we conquer the world?"

"Absolutely," he answered, sinking the bandages in a bucket. A knock on the door interrupted them.

It was Lewis Sylberman -"Your majesty, I heard you were involved in a fight." He said approaching him with curiosity.

"I was."

"Is everything all right?"

"Better than ever," said Leonard offering a glass of whiskey to the Earl. "Leave us, Andrew," He asked, ready to face the traitor.

 Forty

There is potential in momentum, and with new determination, the King strutted across his throne room with confidence. Members of the house looked offended at his derelict behavior, but this was the moment he had always dreamed. He stopped at the center of the room turned to face them, and announced.

"I call the Lords, Barons, and Knights" He cleared his throat. Murmurs began.

"Silence!" Shouted the Speaker of the House.

Leo continued, "I called the Bishops, Abbots, and Earls. All members of this Parliament, all nobles from spirit." He filled his lungs with air, "Raise your conscience; remember your high rank, the high ideals sown by God in your hearts. Remember the reason why you occupy a seat in this venerable enclosure. Your main objective was not to fulfill your personal desires, or to multiply your fortune, or enjoy glory and power," he could feel their eyes upon him- "The reason why you are seated in these ancient chamber is to carry out your duty with honor."

Once more, murmurs could be heard in the room. "Your moral task is to ensure faithful men...." He looked at them, allowing adrenaline to run thru his body like a river of fire. "Men with integrity, rule this powerful kingdom...because," He was interrupted again by murmurs, "Because a divided nation that can't guarantee justice and peace, runs a high risk to perish." He could see the dismay on their faces. Nevertheless, he continued.

"With these ideas in mind and giving you all my trust to rule, I ask you to work together, be one force, and remain loyal to the crown." Now the house was silent, and all the members of the Parliament were trying to read his intentions.

"You, honorable members of the Parliament, must fight corruption at all levels, and remember your noble duty is to protect the future generations." He looked at the house attentively and continued feeling a hole in his stomach. Some members were ready to shout with disgust. His hands were shaking. "Also, remember always to ensure the human dignity of every subject...and rule with justice."

He took a pause, felt a lump in his throat and tried to push back tears. Then he raised his voice. "Standing on my royal prerogative, I am abdicating the throne to my cousin George, Duke of Windelwood."

Everybody stood up, the crowd shouted, but he continued raising his voice- "Also, I proclaimed the Treaty of the Union, where the small nations around us; those that had shown interest in joining the opposition to defeat me, now would have the opportunity to be part of Norland, as one State." He paused again while the Speaker of the House continued making signs for silence.

"This will allow everybody to share taxes, trade, and increase wealth." Suddenly, the house went silent, expecting his next move.

Leo took a deep breath, and with a loud voice finished.

"I will retire with my family to the colonies in the New World,"

Men yelled.

"Silence!" -shouted the speaker of the House again.

Leo cleared his throat and continued, "The Queen and I will move to the colonies, and from there, I'll report to his majesty King George, as Viceroy."

The room went into a commotion. Leo stopped for seconds and took a good look at all his men. Some were staring at him perplexed when he shouted- "Hail the King!"

"HAIL KING GEORGE!" A crowd of angry men yelled with stupor.

"The greater the power, the more dangerous the abuse."
- Edmund Burke.

Forty one

Voyage

"What is inside those trunks?" Andrew asked, standing at the harbor.

"I don't know, Grace packed the entire palace" said the King, cracking a smile while smoking his pipe. With sweetie hands, he took his son in his arms. He had hope for a new life, cheering and bright as his son's smile but, Grace looked devastated, she overloaded the ship with chest and coffers. Her servants were checking carefully that all the trunks were placed inside the vessel.

It was a chilly morning, and the royal family would navigate the Atlantic Ocean for about 65 days towards the New World. At the harbor, some faces were sad, as they hated to see the handsome couple abdicate the throne, but the majority agreed with the idea of the exile. Most of the Kingdom wanted to witness the event.

The aristocrats were dressed elegantly on the farewell day. Many were singing; others were crying.

"Here they are, lovers and haters; friends and enemies, all together for the last time." Observed the former King. They walked inside the ship, and from the stern, they waved goodbye. Pipes were playing and the vessel moved into the open ocean. People were shouting. "God bless the King and Queen of Norland!" And sad feelings invaded the passengers.

"I would probably never see my parents again, or the castle where we met," Grace said, and her eyes watered. Leo held her close to his chest.

"We'll be fine; this is the right thing to do." He kissed her hands and said, "Remember, if together, we are home" -she nodded and squeezed his hands, allowing tears to run through her cheeks. Cannons fired, and the shore disappeared while pipes and drums could be heard at a distance.

"Immense pain is to leave home, a feeling of deep sorrow is to abandon what you love most."

Feared Enemy

"Forty-eight days, Andrew," said Leo, standing on the bow of the ship feeling the ocean breeze on his face.

"At least Grace is feeling better now," noted Andrew.

"She was seasick for so long. I was frightened."

"Still I feel the tension all around us. I had alerted your personal guards," Andrew said peeling an orange with a small knife.

"Frankly, I'm praying for a safe arrival."

Andrew was continually spying, listening to crew conversations. "Do you fear a conspiracy from the new king?" -he asked, finishing the orange.

"Yes," Leo sighed and took a spyglass out of his pocket. "War is in the air, Andrew." He looked at the horizon. Leo turned and walked a few feet. He lowered his voice, "There are a couple of sailors I saw this morning and couldn't recognize them. They looked questionable."

"Describe them."

"One is tall, fair-skinned, middle age, with shoulder-length brown hair. The other is a blond, young. I caught a name… Albert. Find what you can. Use discretion."

Andrew looked for the suspicious couple.

He focused his sight on the stern of the ship, and he found one of the strangers, opening trunks in his master's cabin. He rummaged in the vaults and filled them with stuff to finally push the trunks, both out.

"So that's it?" Andrew thought- "They are thieves!" He considered chasing them down when he realized it wasn't worth calling attention; after all, his master asked for discretion. Andrew went to the guards and ordered the stranger men capture. Soon, the night fell upon the ship lit by torches and candles. Leo decided to walk around with his guards in Andrew's company.

While a lively conversation about the arrest of the bandits; the men passed the stern of the ship, and Leo saw, out of the corner of his eye, a familiar shadow. He walked towards it and froze in an instant. He recognized his all-time enemy. The dreaded Alchemist was facing him with a gun in his hand.

"Don't attempt to move," the man threatened the guards, touching the king's forehead. "We'll be in charge of this trip, Leonardo." He said and forced the king into a cabin. The wizard locked the door and hit the King's guard.

"Open the door. Why did you call me Leonardo? My name is Leonard. Let me out!" -The king shouted, as he saw in terror Grace and Julian being placed in one of the safety boats, and dozen men stepped from behind the bridge.

"Release the Queen!" -Andrew shouted and pointed a pistol at the young man, Albert. The thief was taking the Queen prisoner.

"Move, Andrew!" Shouted the Alchemist.

The King hit the door with his body and freed himself from the cabin, then ran to his wife. In a question of minutes, he was surrounded by mutineers. He fought with a fist, then found a sword and joined the battle.

"Get out of here! Into the boat with your wife!" Shouted the young blond, Albert, who took the King by the shoulder, and the Alchemist got him from his waist.

Both men threw Leo into the ocean. He tried to hold a robe but missed and vaguely saw Andrew get knocked out while he was flying in the air.

"Noooooo!" Leo shouted; next, he swam in the dark and caught the small boat with Grace and Julian. They could hear screams from the ship on fire.

"Row… come on….row away!" -Somebody shouted at him.

Leo didn't return to the ship. He never knew why, but he rowed away as fast as he could. Grace was fighting him for the oars. "What are you doing? Go back to the ship."

A vast explosion silenced her screams suddenly, and they saw parts of the vessel fly and then return to the ocean.

"What happened?" She cried.

"I don't know….an explosion!"

"Where's Andrew…and, my maids?"

The ship caught fire fast and sank in front of their eyes. They didn't move or make any sound, as they were not sure yet what had happened. After some time, Leo started rowing the oars. He was confused and, at the same time, grateful for being in the little boat. The night was quiet, and he tried to see into the waters. He wanted to recognize the burned corpses floating around them; his wife noticed cold blood.

"They're dead…everybody's dead. There are no survivors." A barrel was floating next to them. He attempted to upload it into the boat. But the boat wasn't big enough. "Let it go….let everything go!" She said while reaching her rosary from her dress pocket.

"Mommy, I want water." Said her child.

Leonard looked on the bottom and found a canteen. "Here, give this to Julian. Drink, son." For hours the only sound they could hear was the oars crushing on the vast ocean. "Why are you rowing….where are we going?" Asked his woman, who finally closed her eyes.

"I don't know… mighty God… I don't know where we are," Leo whispered in the dark.

Forty two

Somewhere in the Caribbean Sea
During the 18 Century

Hours after the explosion, a deep discouragement overwhelmed them. The night became intensely dark. Large clouds blocked the stars and made it difficult to have an idea of their location. The moon in a waning quarter barely illuminated with a ray of hope, and the sound of the lapping waves was rocking them. They had to fight to keep their eyes open. "This has to be a conspiracy, orchestrated by Cousin George, Sylberman and probably the Alchemist," the King murmured.

"Does it matter whose fault is this? Where are we, Leonard?

"I'm trying to read the sky."

"You have no idea yet, ah?" said Grace and continued praying her rosary.

"I'm glad we're far away from everybody" Leo thought, and rowed madly upset.

He remembered the prediction. *"There will be a violent encounter with your enemy, this will happen shortly. Damn it...they took Andrew!"* Leo stopped the boat and licked his lips on a canteen.

"What happened, why did we stopped?"

"They captured Andrew!"

"Everybody is dead. Soon, we'll be dead too."

"I don't think he is dead, and I know what I'm doing."

"Sure, Captain black beard, keep rowing in circles."

The monotonous sound of the ocean and the constant movement of the waves lulled them. Grace and the child fell asleep. A tiny moonlight shone in Grace's face; she looked tense. Leo stopped rowing and got close to them. He caressed her face and prayed, *"Oh, Lord don't let us perish here in the middle of the ocean,"* he took the rosary from his wife's hand. After a few hours, fatigue overcame him, and he finally fell asleep too.

Slowly as a worm crossed a backyard, dawn broke in the sky and the next hours felt eternal. The blazing sun forced them to keep their eyes shut. They protect their faces from burning with pieces of cloth that Leo kept wet. Food was not available, and the infant was uneasy until he finally felt unconscious-"Here moisture his leaps." He told his wife, giving her a wet rag.

There was nothing to do but wait for a miracle. Finally, the sun went down. The boat was barely big enough for the three of them; most of the space was occupied by two chests that Grace stubbornly insisted on keeping.

Half asleep, Leo remembered how many times he used to dream about crossing the ocean. He would fantasized about venturing into the new world in search of treasures. Through the years, he heard amazing stories about brave men who sailed to the new world. He secretly envied them and felt nothing could be more liberating than navigating the open ocean. But that horrible night, the reality was far from any dreams of adventure.

"Grace… can you hear me?" He touched one of her legs. His wife didn't respond.

"Are you thirsty?"

"No, save it for the child," she answered with dry lips. Her eyes were closed and her face was pale, almost like a corpse.

"*God have mercy of our souls*!" Leo whispered desperately. His dread was impossible to control. Their destiny was uncertain, the end imminent. He wanted to shout for help, but he knew there was no one to respond to his plea. The tiny boat was floating, isolated in the middle of the ocean. He felt small and vulnerable like an insect in a gigantic pool. Finally, he closed his eyes too and lost track of time. He couldn't say how many hours passed when the sound of a seagull awakened them. They opened their eyes; it was daybreak.

"Land, Grace!" Leo yelled. The beach was in front of them. Surrounded by crystal water like a pool, they could see the bottom of the ocean easily. Grace sat up.

"Row, come on row to the shore," she cried, holding her unconscious son. Leo's laughter echoed on the beach as he rowed frenetically. Safe at the shore, they walked on white sand, fine as sugar. He took the boat up the beach and hid it, secure behind a rock.

Then asked his wife. "Can you walk?" She nodded.

"Where are we?"

"I don't have… the slightest idea," he answered holding her by the waist and carrying the sleepy child on his left shoulder. "Julian's dehydrated. We need water!"

They walked on the beach isolated. Ahead they could see the dancing palms enjoying the beat of the ocean breeze, making the jungle an inviting place. Loud unfamiliar noises could be heard coming from everywhere. Everything was wonderfully alive and green.

Walking thru the jungle, they experienced the strange feeling of being observed. Leo could hear footsteps following them. He turned several times and saw nobody behind them, but bushes and leaves that moved. The air was hot and humid, making breathing difficult. The sounds of nature, locusts, and chipping birds played in the background. It was early in the morning, and Julian was recovering his senses, still in his father's arms. He opened his eyes and called.

"Mommy… Mommy!"

Grace was walking slowly behind them.

"I'm here, baby."

She tried to reach them, so she stopped to remove some clothes that hindered her from walking faster, then placed a large piece of cloth on Julian's head. The sound of running water nearby worked together like mothers earth symphony.

"Freshwater… here!" Cried her husband. A beautiful creek was in front of them. They drank from it and Leo filled his canteen.

He refreshed his son's head with the crystal water, and when he glanced at the area, looking for a cave to provide protection, Grace released a moan. She was standing in a little puddle of liquid coming from his legs.

"Grace!" He held her, and a terrifying feeling invaded them. His wife sat on the ground holding her stomach; she cried painfully, "I think… my fountain broke,"

"What?"

"I am in….LABOR."

Leo became pale- "Are you sure?"

"Yes…ahhhh…"

"Oh, Lord….What can I do?"

"Bring some linens…and…ahhhhh….GOD." She bent.

"Do you mean you're delivering …here…now?"

"YES!" She yelled with watery eyes.

"Linens? Stay here…Don't move! I'll be right back….*Bloody time,"* -he thought.

His wife sat on the grass and Julian began to cry, acknowledging his mother's pain "MOMMY!"

"Stay, son. Stay here, don't move, I'll be right back." The young father ran to the beach where he left the boat and opened one of the chests. The first chest was full of clothes and shoes. Leo dumped the clothing to the ground, and moaned a curse, *"Women!"*

He opened the second box, then felt a rush of adrenaline as he looked through the contents. It was full of useful goods; he took a knife, a big sheet, and clothes for the baby. Then returned to his wife as fast as he could. Upon seeing Grace, he stopped in one jump. Grace was in labor, her face was blushed, her forehead was drenched in sweat, and her eyes were tightly shut. "Water!"-she cried. He immediately, ran to the creek. When collecting the water, he saw a native coming from the jungle and approaching her to lift her over his shoulders.

"NO!" -Leo shouted, took Julian and ran after the stranger yelling at him. "PUT HER DOWN, YOU… PUT HER DOWN RIGHT NOW!!!"

But the little man didn't stop. On the contrary, he ran faster into the jungle. Leonard's heart was pumping so fast; he thought, he might have a heart attack. He was certain the native would kill

Grace but the guy stopped suddenly, looked back at him smiled, and threw the Queen into a deep crystal lake next to a waterfall.

"GRACE!" A shudder ran through his body. His immediate reaction was to save his wife, so he placed his son on a high rock and took off his coat. The little prince stood atop of the rock, weeping loudly. His body was trembling and his eyes were full of tears. He was hugging the piece of cloth his mom gave him; his only possession and comfort at that moment. Unable to speak, he finally gasped. "PAPAA!"

As he saw his father dive in the water, causing a big splash from the lake.

Forty three

Sacred Waters of Chaac's Lake

Leo jumped into the lake with a knife in his mouth; swimming deep, he witnessed the most unusual and amazing sight. As Grace sank into the bottomless blue of the pond, the baby was born in the deepest part of the lake. The little creature started to sink too. Leo opened his eyes wild and observed such a miracle perplexed.

"How the hell is this possible?"

He swam to his wife, and with the knife, cut the umbilical cord. The newborn infant seemed to breathe in the shallow depths of the lake, her eyes were wide open, and her legs moved contently like a sea turtle. Leo noticed Grace was sinking and took her in his arms. With a rapid move, he grabbed the baby and swam as fast as he could to the surface.

He placed his wife next to a rock and comforted her, "Easy, darling...breathe, just breathe."

Grace coughed until she could normally breathe again. Then removed some of her wet clothes and asked, "How's the baby? Is he alive?" Leo took a deep breath and cried with emotion, "She's fine....IT'S A GIRL!" -He said and took the piece of cloth from Julian's hand to cover the child in his arms.

After a few seconds, Leo took a glance at the place. Julian was standing high over the rock, not moving a muscle. The young father saw the little boy's eyes and mouth wide open while staring at the native, whose face was painted white and red. Almost naked, the native only was wearing a type of loincloth. The family rested their eyes on him without moving a muscle. He exchanged looks with them, trying to guess what would happen in the following seconds. All types of thought crossed Leo's mind. But there was no sign of violence anywhere. The native was a boy, maybe a teenager, with a smirk forming across his painted face. They looked at each other with curiosity.

Leo glanced at the jungle; he dared to walk a few steps, moving with precaution. His forehead was sweating, and his heart was pounding with the possibility of a surprise attack from a native tribe.

But the palms were moving in a magnificent dance to the rhythm of the wind. There was any sigh of human trace. The sounds of the jungle were interrupted when the native suddenly let out a laugh. The little man was jumping and dancing comically, expressing joy. Stress blew up as Leo couldn't hold his spirit anymore and let out a hysterical laugh mirroring the native and his wife, who was also chuckling incoherently.

Sweet flower

The new baby in Leonard's arms cried loudly and interrupted the celebration. Leo felt an incredible pride holding his newborn. Dad's copycat, an absolute fingerprint of his- "She's gorgeous," he exclaimed.

"Let me see," Grace requested, trying to reach them.

"Don't move, darling," he placed the baby in her arms. The Lady could hardly speak after the commotion, and found it difficult to move from the rock.

"She's like a little flower," she murmured. The excitement of having her daughter in her arms calmed her immediately. She was immersed in a warm feeling, and the harshness of the environment vanished like magic.

"You need dry clothes!" Leo observed.

"I'm fine," she answered, smiling to her husband with a peaceful warmth he hadn't seen in a long time. The native got closed to them and started taking in his language; Leo finally lowered his guard and showed the young man the new baby, "It's my daughter!" He said proudly. Julian stepped carefully down the rock. He sobbed and smiled with traces of tears on his face.

"Here little fellow, meet your sister." Said Leo and carried his son. "We just witnessed a miracle," Grace told, him embracing both children.

Leo nodded, "Praise the Lord!" His eyes watered.

"I thought we'd die in the boat," she confessed and kissed Julian.

"We're safe and sound by God's grace," affirmed Leo, feeling grateful. An instant of comfort captured them while fine rain fell like a refreshing shower covering the island with steam.

Forty Four

The island, tropical and humid, had virtually two seasons. Located south of the Tropic of Cancer, the rainforest was rich in vegetation. The jungle-covered dozens of acres across the island that perched on a hilltop resembling a soft green cloak.

"Where are we, Leonard?"

"I don't know," he answered and walked around. Despite the tremendous humidity and heat, the scenery was spectacular. The former King wanted to communicate with the native. The boy looked to be in his middle teens probably 14. A peculiar birthmark, similar to a half-moon was on his right cheek. They boy seemed to have some type of disability as he acted childishly. His entire body was covered in scars and bruises. His hands and feet were small. His eyes were almond shaped, and his face round, connected to a very short neck. Leonard had seen this kind of child before. Some kingdoms killed them at birth, claiming they were sons of trolls or witches.

In his former kingdom, they were considered good people but slow, and many live in monasteries.   Grace never saw someone like him. The native aroused his wife's fear to the point that she was not able to be near him.

After telling him everybody's names and explaining they were peaceful people. The native finally produced clear sounds, and they interpreted his name as Ozxei-Lui-Ha. Leonard tried to tell him his name, "I'm Leonard." But the boy shook his head and called him "Papa," mirroring Prince Julian.

"I wish I could understand him," Leo told Grace.

"He talks and talks without listening."

"Indeed, he reminds me of some Lords in Parliament and your mother."

"Oh, for God's sake!" She sound tired.

"Can you walk?"

"Yes, but where? Where do you want to go?"

"I don't know, the native wants to show me something?" he told her, and with renewed strength, they walked after Ozxei. Half of a mile into the wilderness they found something similar to a shelter-a deteriorated hut where the native boy lived. Apparently, the island was inhabited. When this finally hit Leo, it was like a hundred-ton load had just been dropped onto his head. They were living a precious venture probably too risky to survive. "We might be alone in the island," he said to Grace who was barefoot.

"I need some shoes. Please bring my things," she asked and sat on a rock. Leo brought the chests to the native's hut, with the native's help, who followed him everywhere like a shadow.

"Open them, I'm excited," asked his wife.

The young husband noticed some wild goats running towards the native. He pointed at them and asked-"Hey! Boy, are these your goats?.... Hey!"

"Come on Leonard, the native can't understand you…open the chests!" Grace was sweating copiously.

"We can use some goat milk!" He said optimistically.

She glared at him impatiently, "Oh, my my…this heat!"

"Here, drink from the canteen. Let's see. What we have here… there… eh… this is my pipe and tobacco!"

"Cooking pans, scissors, MATCHES." Noticed Grace.

"Rope, an AXE…. Remarkable!

"Oh, God's Heaven, where are my things?" Grace moaned desperately.

"Binoculars, pistol, and ammunition. Wow…candles," Leo was excited.

"Who packed all this rubbish?" Said Grace, moodily jumping onto the chest.

"You dear. Can't remember?"

"Oh, wait…these are some shoes, a mirror, and a hairbrush."

"You can't wear those shoes here, they're useless."

"Hush….Look. Clothes for the baby, and blankets," she finally smiled. "This has to be a tea seat. Oh! This… box… I recognize this box….there," she opened a silver box adorned with gems "Gold coins and MY JEWELS!"

"Ha, jewels, just what I need on a desert island."

Grace glanced at him, upset.

"Paper, and ink. I can write a survival journal, absolutely fantastic."

"Sure be the author of… *Adventures of a castaway King and his native savage.*"

"You hush…look nails: a hammer, a fishing net, and a bible." Leonard stood perplexed, wondering how his wife could have come up with the idea of packing all those convenient, but otherwise unrelated items. He exclaimed, pleased, "These are all our possessions. Some items are valuable."

"Valuables? With some exceptions, nothing but rubbish! There are so many things we need!" The young mother padded with clothes the bottom of the wooden box, and gently placed the baby inside.

"Grace, I fear for our safety; we might not be alone, after all," he did not want to tell her, but he had to.

"What do you mean?"

"I think I saw the Alchemist on the ship," he closed the second chest, sat on it, and lighted up his pipe, "I'm sure he blew up the ship." The native was eating the remains of a grilled iguana and he offered a bit to Grace.

"NO!" She shook her head, "I don't think the Alchemist is a problem. There are no survivors; all died."

"We don't know," Leo accepted the bite, "Thanks…mmm…guess what it tastes like…?

"It tastes like chicken,"

"No, it tastes like iguana…ha.ha.ha."

She crunched- "Ah!" and touched her stomach. "What have I done? I'm condemned by my sins," she said and ran to a bush to vomit.

"What's going on, woman? Here drink some water."

She coughed loudly, vomited again, and finally accept a drink of water. "Why?" She cried

"Don't have to eat it if you don't want to."

She nodded and confessed, "I'm so miserable….before we married, I stole my grandfather's chest containing all the Alchemist potions and books," she continued, "I went to a witch and asked her to prepare the same potion they gave you."

"What?" -He interrupted- "You never told me this."

"Can't you guess?"

"Guess what. Do you mean you?"

"Yes…me…Julian…and the newborn."

"We all are….." Leo was shocked.

"CURSE…CAN'T YOU SEE…WE ARE CURSED!" She shouted hysterically.

"I can't believe this…why you do things without consulting me?"

"Now, we ALL are going to live for a thousand years, lost in this bloody island. With no food, no place to live, in the hands of A SAVAGE, PROBABLY… A CANNIBAL!"

"Calm down," The idea of being lost and isolated was unbearable. At that moment, he wasn't ready for the challenge. Suddenly, the native ran to Leo, pushed him, and shouted- "KAN, KAN!" He pointed at a huge snake hanging on a tree, ready to bite Grace. Leo took the reptile by the head and threw it against some rocks, bouncing his head and killing it in an instant.

"Look out!" Grace shouted. A spider, the size of a fist, approached them. Leo crushed the insect with his boot. His wife was standing next to him, pale, unable to say a word. Their new home was a wild, desolate island full of crawling things that could kill in an instant.

"Was that a spider?" She finally reacted.

"Yes, it was, a huge one," he whispered, hidden his concern.

"We're not going to survive here!"

"Yes, we will," Leo held Grace next to him, while the native continued taking in his language.

"Acceptance. Good and bad, fortune and misfortune,
Pleasure and pain, I want it all, because it's mine!"
- Innocent Mwatsikesimbe.

Forty Five

After two days of being in the shore burning touches, the former King had his skin red and his spirit cast down. While he gained some confidence in developing survival skills, his wife sank in melancholy. They didn't know Grace was suffering a case of post part reaction. She was irritable, anxious, and muddy by the constant presence of the native boy who followed them everywhere.

Oxie, as Leo called him, showed them how to dry fish and fruits, hanging from sticks next to a smoky bonfire. But Grace didn't pay him any attention; she walked on the beach instead, playing with the white sand and stared at the horizon without uttering a word, while she rocked her new born in her arms.

"Look, I found some bananas, there are small, but good," said Leo, sitting next to a bonfire.

"I'm not hungry. I can't stop thinking about my family. Probably they think we're dead."

"Probably."

"You don't care…don't you?"

Leonard offered her fruit and said, "I care. Please eat." But she walked away. "Grace, you've hardly eaten. You need nourishment," he insisted. Julian ran to him. "Here, have a banana, son," the infant sat on his lap and ate with appetite.

"Soon, it will be the feast of Saint Gregory, our Patron Saint," she noticed walking away from them, "We'll miss the procession, the service, all the chants. I love the choir so much," she said with watery eyes.

The sun was setting. The new baby in Grace's arms began to cry, and she sang an old hymn,

"Oh dear father, cheer our way, with Thy love's perpetual ray. Grant us every closing day," she stared at the ocean. Tears ran down her face, "Holy Spirit, be thou night, when in mortal pains we lie. Grants us as we come to die," she chocked up emotion.

"Grace, I beg. Don't duel in pain."

Julian ran to her, trying to console; he shared the rest of his fruit.

"Thank you, baby."

Leo grabbed some things and exclaimed, "Is getting late. Let's go back to the shelter."

"You call that hovel a shelter?"

"I'm thinking of building a better one."

They walked back to the jungle. The native was talking and making body signs. Leo asked Grace, "Do you think we can teach him to speak our language?"

She nodded.

"Maybe I can start teaching him some basic words; I want to give him a new name."

"He already has a name."

"A name I can't pronounce…Oxzi- lu -ha- ra.. ra… can you?"

"Poor kid, he's not normal. Who could abandon someone like him, on a desolated island?"

"He had survived," Leo observed, cracking a smile, "He yells madly when I don't understand him."

Grace felt the eyes of the young native looking at her with awe, making her blush and felt awkward. She tried to ignore him, but the orphan stared at her, insistently. Finally she settled her eyes on him, and saw deep sorrow in those black pearls. He looked defenseless and innocent. Her fear diminished.

Then she said to her husband, "Jordy!"

"What is that?"

"Call him Jordy. Short for Gregory."

"Like the Patron?"

"Well, thanks to him we're surviving," she noticed.

Her husband liked the idea. He walked towards the boy and rested his hand on the native's chest, "Boy. I want to call you… Jordy." The guy smiled at him and tried to repeat the name…"J..o…d..y"

"Yes…Jordy… he likes it!"

"Good!" Grace said.   She gave Leo the newborn, turned around, and walked indifferently.

"Where are you going?"

"Back to the shore."

"It's late. We've been hours looking for a vessel." She didn't listen. "Grace, if together, at home we are. Remember?"

"Don't give me your bloody crap!" And she ran back to the shore.

He shouted at her, "IT'S DANGEROUS OUT THERE, I NEED YOU HERE WITH THE CHILDREN."

He ran after her, and managed to hold her by the arm, but she pushed him away, "Don't you touch me; I don't want you near me. Everything, it's your damn fault. You escaped your obligations and ran away from your responsibilities. I don't want to see your face no more," and she disappeared into the forest.

A couple of hours later she returned with scraped knees and mud on her feet. Julian was sleeping, and the newborn was in

Leo's arms. She walked over to her son and kissed him. Then took the baby and walked slowly around the hut. She finally placed the girl inside the wooden box.

"Find anything new?"

"No," she responded and took her husband's knife, stared at him with rancor- "You should kill us all tonight, while we sleep."

He removed the knife from her hands, "Stop climbing trees; you can hurt yourself!" -He said irritably- "Go to bed. It's late."

"The fairy tale is over, Leonard. Accept it! There is no more King or Queen, or Kingdom," she said and stared at him.

"You need rest," he lay down next to her and closed his eyes, listening to the last pieces of wood that crackled in the fire.

Soon, he remembered how happy she was in their castle and wished, he could somehow artificially recreate her joy. He recalled her smile, the sun reflecting on her golden hair. The way the breeze treed and danced with her gaunt. He was lifting her off her feet high in the air, her ecstatic laughter echoed in the Castle, and then just like that, something dropped to the ground with a loud THUD!

He awoke suddenly, and barely had time to realize he was dreaming. He examined what could have possibly made that noise and walked outside the hut, ducking through the small entrance. He noticed a coconut had fallen from a palm and hit a piece of bark. It had barely dented. He picked up the fruit and looked down to see if anything else had fallen; a few pots laid in the sand in disarray. He noticed footprints leading towards the jungle, and felt alarmed. What if there had been someone there? What if the coconut had actually startled an intruder?

"No is Grace, she woke up...." then he remembered his youngsters and his wife's threat of killing them. He rushed back to the hut. He panicked, looked for Julian, but he was soundly asleep. In one jump, he hung on the wooden box -he turned out with ease.

Dry flowers fell slowly to the ground. The baby was gone.

He ran to the lake. Grace was walking with the baby girl half body inside the lagoon. He grabbed her by the shoulder and tried to stop her. "Where are you going?"

Her eyes were red, with traces of tears on her face.

She didn't answer. An empty look was on her face as if she was hypnotized.

"Darling, stop....get out of the lake."

"I cannot take care of this child."

"Darling, give me the baby. Sit here, let me hold you."

"Where are we? What is this nation? Are we going to survive?"

"Yes...yes..." he checked the sleeping baby and kissed her.

"I'm so weak. The food is horrendous."

"Your clothes are wet. Let's go back to the shelter."

"There so much work to do. I hardly take care of myself."

He stared at her, "Listen, Grace….You're not alone…..I'm with you!"

"Take me out of here; I hate this place."

"Darling, rely on me…God is with us….look at the native."

"The poor savage….he is a kid…just a kid."

"He is a proven miracle!"

She cried bitterly. He took her face in his hands.

"I'll found a place to build a new hut, a better one and…. I'll find the way to take you back to civilization. I promise."

"Oh, Leonard. Can't you see? We lost everything. Fortune, assets, friends. Everything."

"No, we didn't lose everything." He kissed the child in her arms tenderly. The baby opened her mouth. She was hungry. Both parents smiled at her.

"I've been thinking to name her after your mother."

"Victoria?" The thought made her smile.

"Yes, Victoria."

"It's a good name." She sobbed.

Gentle breeze blew from the ocean, the night was humid and a moonbeam shone on the lake, causing a calming effect. "Come on, let's go to bed. You need to rest," he said and they walked back in silence, but Leo was concerned. He was scared of Grace's reaction. *"I have to find a way. A way to get back to Norland, before we all fly crazy."* He thought.

He couldn't sleep for several nights. The baby was constantly waking them to be fed, and he spent weeks being at the shore for hours looking for a ship. One night, almost at the crack of dawn, he confronted his denial; he came to the conclusion that rescue was not going to happen. His kingdom was gone, sunken, vanished forever.

There was no use trying to reclaim it. There was no possible exit of the present circumstance.

Sitting on a trunk, with a full moon shining in the sky and everybody sleeping; he covered his head with his hands and allowed himself to cry like a child. He had to free himself from the pain and deception. Heal, reborn, or everybody would perish with him. He walked barefoot and looked at the sky, then shouted with arms in the air, "GOD, WHERE ARE YOU!!" his voice echoed in the shadows as he fell on his knees on the ground.

"Fire test gold, suffering test brave men."
- Seneca

Forty six

2 months, 3 weeks, 6 days after the shipwreck.

After a family effort, a new shelter was finished. On top of a hill where they could see most of the west side of the island. Their new home had a breathtaking view of jungle and the beach.

"How do you like it?" Asked Leo exited.

"I love it. I like the size, it's so comfortable." She observed, arranging her hair with a flower in front of a little mirror.

"More important…it's a safety spot!" He noticed, enjoying the view. The hut was simple. Constructed mainly of wood. It had a thatched roof made with dry palms. Outside, there was a pond to store fresh fish and a pit to cook. Inside, there was a bed made with a base of wood; dry leaves, and feathers covered with goat fur.

Hammocks for Julian and Jordy were at the back, separated with a partition made with bamboo and shells. A basket functioned as a baby crib was suspended from the ceiling next to their bed. It was filled with tropical flowers, and the infant was in the middle babbling and playing with her feet, "My little princess," he caressed the baby.

"Victoria," her mother called her lovingly. "Come baby!"

Leo was satisfied; his castle was unconventional but efficient. Grace took the baby girl and stepped outside, feeling proud of their hard work and commitment. Leo followed her and held her by her waist.

"The sight is magnificent," she noticed. The waves were singing and the breeze of the sea washed into their faces with a sense of a deep calm and paradise beauty.

"This is your new castle, milady."

"I'll be thrilled to see a sunrise from here, every morning," she said eagerly.

"A majestic symphony conducted by luminous Sol; where the birds sing their first song, and hundreds of flowers release their perfume. In your honor, queen of my castle and pain in my neck," he said and bowed.

"Ha, better than pain in the ass," she pushed him away and went back inside. Although a little more positive, Grace continued showing signs of depression. Her troubled mind was full of nostalgia, and she got irritable, distracted, and sometimes moody. Leo was kind and warm-hearted. For her luck, her husband was a steadfast man with fortitude. At the door, he grabbed her arm and called her attention.

"Milady….see what Jordy and I found for your supper." Leo showed the pond.

"Are those lobsters? They're huge."

"We'll have a special supper tonight." He offered her an open coconut. "Cheers to our castle!"

"Cheers."

"You don't remember, do you?" He asked, surprised.

"Yes, I do. Today is our anniversary."

"And…I have a surprise for you."

"Let me guess…a delightful dinner of seafood, fresh veggies, and fruits. We will sit around the fire, enjoying the cool breeze of the night."

"Indeed, but there's more." He looked behind a palm and brought two sacks. From one, he pulled out a handmade guitar made with coconut husks.

"Is that a guitar?" She covered her mouth- "I call that a wit!"

"Listen to this…my respectable audience. I'm pleased to present for your entertainment… some music and verses dedicated to your honor."

Grace clapped excitedly, "Julian….Jordy…come! Sit next to me….we'll enjoy the function."

"These simple verses," Leo continued playing, "My simple song I said, might put you in a mood for little dance, but please notice…" Leo played some notes, "I'm a King, not a jester."

"Oh! We don't mind," she clapped, and he felt rewarded.

"From the bottom of my heart. This fairy tale is beginning, milady." Sweet melody came from the instrument, and Leo sang in his remarkable low voice.

I come to you,

To see your eyes,

To find your smile,

My private paradise,

Baby, darling, tell me

Can you see the ocean?

Can you to hear the birds?

He furnished flower wreaths from the second sack and adorned every head, including Jordy's, who was clapping, showing his contagious smile.

"Flower wreaths…lovely," noticed his wife touching her head.

You are probably sighing,
In a lost past,
A sweet illusion,
Fairyland of the mind.

You and I,

Vagabonds in the land,
We barely make it,
Miles apart,
While everything that matters.
Banished in the dark,

Baby, darling, tell me
Would you like to hear the birds?
Would you allow the ocean waves?
To heal the pain.

Because tomorrow is a wish,
Yesterday is lost in the wind,
Allow me to be part of this moment
Together we shall find
A new castle, a new kingdom
A new way,
To be again.

Leo bowed to his audience. The group laughed and clapped.

"And now, a gift….for the Queen of the castle."

"Is there more? I'm excited!"

He pulled out a basket and presented it to her. She looked at the contents both confused and delighted, "It's a set of brushes and paints!"

"I made them with Jordy's help. We managed to concoct by crushing flowers and bugs." She looked at him overwhelmed. He asked eagerly, "Can you paint me a sunset?" She ran to him and hugged him, "I never had so much in my life!"

Leonard's tender care and love were more than enough to feel alive again.

"We're in a paradise, and you and my children are my treasure," she said kissing him back. That night, they cooked together, danced and sang old tunes, until late.

The next day, Grace went to the beach in a different mood. She allowed the ocean breeze to blow in her body. She was where she was supposed to be; her affliction vanished.

A new vision conquered her heart; she was free to be herself. There was no court to please, or rancid aristocracy to fear. She was away from the corruption of greed, away from the desire for power that only creates hatred and suspicion among men. Away of aristocrats living in a world without substance, wearing makeup faces and fine clothes to cover their emptiness and sorrow.

Barefoot, she ran and connected with sand and the ocean. She felt the energy and beauty of nature blooming around her. She lost her clothes, and splashed in the ocean naked, laughing and singing like a girl. Her heart was joyful, her spirit free; full of simple happiness that would endure for the rest of her life and make her strong like a steel warrior.

Treasure Island

For the young father, living on a forsaken island was an extreme challenge. Accustomed to a life of comfort and luxury, surrounded by servants; now he had to fight for survival. After the hard labor involved in the construction of the hut. Leo had more time to reflect and develop his fishing and hunting skills. The place was home to the most vivid colored reefs and ocean fauna they had ever seen. In those three months, Leo's heart changed as well as his appearance. Now, his hair fell to his shoulder. His beard and mustache were thick and long. His body was tanned and muscular, covered with blisters and cuts that little by little were healing. Against odds, his back pain decreased. He was thankful to The Providence for Jordy. Together, father and son used the morning to fish while in the afternoons, they were forced to cover from the rough sun and stay indoors. Sometimes, frustration conquered Leo. However, from time to time, he cracked a smile with the thought of not having to work long hours at the Parliament anymore. After all, he proved he was still King. Master of his island as most men are, with or without crown, throne, or Parliament. He still ruled, provided, and protected his little tribe like a lion in a jungle.

One afternoon, while sitting on the beach, Leo marveled at seeing his daughter passionately trying to capture the ocean in her little hands. Jordy was clapping happily with his unique zest for life, while Julian was jumping at every wave that touched his bare feet.

"They are blooming like flowers in a garden," he noticed to his wife, sitting next to him. The tropical sun and humid weather increased Grace's beauty to an exceptional level.

Now, her body was stronger than ever, her long curly hair was falling on her back like a golden cascade. Her pale figure was replaced by a perfect suntan making her blue eyes glitter like sapphires.

"Can you believe this sunset?" She asked Leo.

"Indeed," he answered, and thought –"*God is in every spot in this island.*" Ocean and sky blended together with a symphony of oranges, vibrant reds, and soft purples. The rhythmic sound of the waves was mesmerizing and the smell of the sea brought fresh particles of life in it. They were captivated by the moment and forgot the calamities of life, in an isolated place near to the heart of heaven and beyond the forbidden sea. They discovered a treasure, where moments of bliss were possible.

"On Earth There Is No Heaven,
But There Are Pieces of It."
- Jules Renard

 Forty seven

4 months, 2 weeks, 3 days, after the shipwreck.

"Today, I officially start a new expedition to the jungle," Leo said after breakfast, wearing a straw hat- "There is a vast amount of jungle that needs my attention."

"You shall give your attention to the coast behind those mountains." Grace complained.

"Darling, not an inch of the island will be ignore by the expedition, but today is the time to go deep into the jungle, right Jordy?" said Leo, as he grabbed his knife and cane.

"BE SAFE AND COME BACK FOR SUPPER!" Grace shouted to them standing at the entrance of the shelter, while Julian and Vicky waved goodbye to the enthusiastic scouts.

Soon, they were deep into the jungle, through a thriving rainforest. Gargantuan trees towered over them and provided shade from the hundred degrees ardent sun. As they walked, rays of light trickled through immense green leaves, illuminating their path with magical splendor. The unbearable weather made Leo sweat while the rascal ran through the terrain with incredible ability leaping through the trees with ease and vigor.

Jordan's survival story was amazing, not only because of his obvious disability but for the puzzling mystery behind his isolation. Leo couldn't figure out how he survived his tribe, with no war trace, or who could abandon such an innocent young man with a noble spirit.

When they arrived at the top of a hill, an extraordinary valley unfolded before their eyes. It was a green velvet carpet with fruit trees, creeks, and natural traps. Long-tails colorful parrots flew over the valley, giving the impression of a living rainbow. The view was absolutely fantastic. At that moment, an inspiring idea lit up Leo.

"Oh, Lord," he exclaimed breadless. "I've been looking for a reason, a goal to feel alive and gain my will, and you answered my prayers with this..." He muttered to himself running down the hill. "JORDY!!!" He shouted. "We found ....the perfect spot." Leo hugged him bracingly.

"GOD MUST LIKE GOLF, SON!"

Candle on the Ocean

Leo stormed into his home with a pounding heart. He knew a man with imagination is never alone or defeated, so he explained his idea to his wife.

"Hold on, let me understand. Do you think you can build a golf course?"

"Absolutely, and we can make our own clubs and balls."

"That's impossible, absurd, and a waste of energy and time."

"Nothing is impossible, and golf is not a waste of time. Darling, you have to see the place, it's fantastic. We'll build the course around the clearings. We don't have to do much, maybe cut down some trees and…."

"LEONARD, SHOUT UP! I'm not engaging in an exhausting task that will take weeks, maybe months. We're looking for an exit from this place. You promised me to explore the island."

"THAT'S WHAT I JUST DID!"

"The other side of the island. You went to the wrong place."

"Oh, you want to see what is behind the mountains, right?"

"Yes, I've heard noises. It could be ships."

"When did you hear noises?"

"Leonard!" she dropped her voice and stared at him.

"All right, all right. We do it today."

"Today? …the day is almost over."

"We'll do it by boat. I'll take torches."

"And the kids?"

"Jordy can keep an eye on them."

"No, we can't leave them alone." She said, concerned.

"They're having naps. We have at least a couple of hours. It's now or never, Grace."

"Then, get the touches," She didn't hesitate. A deep omen was bordering her, and she couldn't postpone it anymore. They embarked while the sun was setting and walked along the beach where they had never been before. Leo didn't want to miss the opportunity he was longing for, so he stopped and kissed her with passion.

"Alone…at last!"

"Oh, stop it."

"You cannot escape, young lady," he stared at her and hold her by her waist.

"We're here to explore, remember?" She pushed him away.

"You're mine tonight; I going to explore you."

Grace ignored him and ran back to the ocean,

"Where are you going, fool?" He shouted.

She was giggling playing with the warm water. A sky of fire surrounded them. He reached her and said, "There is no perfect moment to love you, like now."

"Do you want me?"

"I'm burning as this firefly sky."

By listening to him, she opened her lips eagerly. Their mouths joined. Next, she jumped, anchoring her legs around his waist. Incredible freedom overwhelmed them. The sound of the ocean was mesmerizing. The soft breeze pursued deranged intimacy. Suddenly, they felt everything was possible. He kissed her shoulder, next to her ear. Grace felt hunger for his tanned and muscular husband, so she didn't think twice; they were lost with excitement. Thousands of stars appeared in the sky and witnessed the lovers.

They got intimate until a big wave splashed, and both arrived to climax, in a final contraction. For a few seconds, they stayed quiet on the sand, breathless admiring the firmament. Leo broke the silence, and said feeling a shock of bliss. "Look at the starts…"

"Beautiful," she whispered, "They're moving to the right."

"It's a dance. Do you remember our first night?" he incorporated under an arm and kissed her. "Thank you, darling, thank you for making me so happy." They kissed again. At that moment a tiny light appeared on the horizon, right in the middle of the sea, then disappeared. Like pulled by a spring, they quickly sat up and wondered what it was; a few minutes later the light reappeared.

"Is it possible? That has to be," she noticed, getting dressed.

"A LIGHTHOUSE! It can't be. That cannot be," shouted Leo.

"Of course. It is," she said excited, "I told you to explore on this site." She jumped into the boat laughing, "Oh, sweet Lord. There is sunshine after rain, yes, there is."

"Bloody island!" Leo said in awe and also jumped into the boat.

 Forty eight

Habanera

After a small argument with Jordy about clothes and shoes, the two men navigated towards the east. A few hours later, in front of their eyes appeared one of the busiest ports they'd ever seen. The aroma of fresh oak, baked bread, fish, spices, and wine was all over the place. The port was mainly a trading spot where ships from the seas stored and collected all type of merchandise. Wine, sugar, coffee, tobacco, and cocoa were acquired by trading gold, jewels, or black slaves. "Let's find someone to talk to" -Leo told Jordy while walking down. The former King was hosting the possibility of finding Andrew alive.

Although, people were talking in different dialects. He noticed Spanish was the prominent language.

"La taberna, donde está la taberna caballero?" - Leo asked and a few minutes later, they were at *Perro Negro*, the local tavern, where the air was thick with fumes of tobacco, beer, and rum.

"I'm looking for a man called Andrew. A sailor wrecked not long ago, from a Norland ship," -Said Leonard to the keeper.

"Ahoy! Who wants to know about good Andrew?" -Asked a man with red hair pulled back, on dirty seaman's clothing with a breaded beard.

"Do you know him….where I can find him?"

"Ha! You look familiar…are you the Old King of Norland?"

"No, I'm not…you idiot," -Leo slammed his beer on the counter. All eyes were fixed on them, and a group of pirates' surrounded them.

"Governor…..don't get excited!" -An old man approached them and touched Leo's shoulder. He noticed Leo's hand on his revolver.

"My name is John. My friends call me Red. Let us alone," – he said to the group around them and moved to a table in the corner. "So, you are not the King?"

"I said I am not. Does this hole have a name?"

"This is Habanera Island, and Andrew is not here, as you can see…."

"Ay."

"Tell me, what is your affair in this land?" -Red asked and took a sip looking at them with flashing eyes.

"I need to know how far we are from the colonies."

"Not far, sun marks on your face, accompanied by a native, you are shipwrecked." -He noticed and scratched his chin.

"True."

"Aye... This is Spanish territory. We are two days away from the colonies, the problem is…"

"What?"

"There's a war…."

"A war?"

"You see..."-He lowered his voice, "The colonies want their independence... from the King" -The man finished his drink.

"A revolt?"

"This is more than a revolt. People are fighting for their freedom," The old man chuckled.

Leo blushed, then asked. "Freedom from the King. Is that possible?" For years Leo was indoctrinated on his divine right to rule. A right deriving from God's will.

"Aye, the idiot raised the taxes." -Answered the pirate, and wiped sweat from his face with a handkerchief- "The colonies refused to pay. Governor, my ship is ready to sail. A beauty she is. We join the French army. Right now, this afternoon!" -The man stood up.

"The French?"

"The allies."

"Oh. No, not today, I'm looking for the rest of my crew-"Leonard tensed, the idea of fighting Northland was unbearable-"First I need to get some supplies."

"Supplies? Have you found a treasure, Governor?"

Leo stood up, looked at the pirate with caution, and then paid for his drink with a golden coin from his pouch.

"We're leaving" -He pushed Jordy out and made him walk fast to the market. "We better get out this rat hole."

Back in his boat, he was meditative; the idea of Andrew's death saddened him, as well as the war news. What was the best thing to do? Maybe go back to Norland. He wasn't sure.

Inside the tavern, Red was talking to his friends. "That bastard found a treasure. I saw his pouch full of gold" -He was flipping the coin from Norland with the image of Leonard in one side. The waiter caught the coin and told the pirates.

"That was the king! I'm sure."

"Ha, ha, ha. That hobo?" The men laughed.

"Get out...there is no free buzz here"

"We better follow him. King or beggar. I'm sure... he's good news."-The group of pirates laughed and looked for Leonard in the crowd.

Forty nine

Island of the Parrots

For Grace and the children, Leo's return from Habanera was a festivity. "Condiments, rice, and….are these?" She held small tin boxes next to her chest.

"Yes…the almond sweets you love."

"Oh, Leonard!"

"In my next trip, I'm planning to get some hens and a roster."

"I need fabric, and tea."

"Mmm" -He smiled pleased.

"Soap and spices!" -She continued.

 "Make a list, darling."

"Why did you bring so little?"-She said savoring the candy.

"We couldn't stay long."

"Why?" -Leonard held her hands and told her calmly, "There's a war in the colonies,"

"A war?"

"The colonies are fighting for their freedom, and a pirate almost recognized me."

"Oh!" -A combination of sorrow and resignation overwhelmed them as they decided to prolong their stay. To earn cash, the King captured parrots to sell. The fantastic 20 inch long birds called Cuban Macaw. Sophisticated and rare birds that draw the attention of aristocrats and wealthy people around the world. The exotic animals soon were of high value in Habanera. Leo and Jordy would make two monthly trips to gather supplies and trade their cages full of Macaw.

Heaven sent angels that are special

Finally, Jordy's mystery was solved. He was abandoned by his tribe as a tribute to their gods. He belonged to the Marabarut people that lived far away from the island, and Jordy through Grace into the lake to save her from pain, as he thought the lake had magic powers.

"Wow, so he was offered to the gods." Grace noticed, preparing dinner.

"Yes, and he tried to help you. I understand him better now."

"He's so sweet. I was so afraid of him when we arrived, and now I love him as my own."

"Of course, what else we can do with someone so innocent and vulnerable." He said, while finishing a golf ball.

"He is more than that, he's like a source of… love."

"Oh, yes…Jordy is nothing but a honey lamb."

"And he's helping you with your crazy dream, how's your golf course coming?"

"It's ready!" Leo exclaimed proudly, "And, Jordy is going to play with papa." He said, smiling.

The two men worked hard on Leo's project.   They cut trees and mowed grass, and by the fourth week, a real golf course began to appear out of the thick jungle. They dug bunkers and filled them out with sand from the beach.

By the middle of the sixth week, Leo and Jordy walked to the first tee, for the pride debut round, on the nine-hole course that turned out to be the gem in the Treasure Island.

Fifty

Curse of Pirates

It was a humid and hot morning when Grace was running up the hill. Her heart was pumping fast. Her hands were sweating; the leaves of the tropical plants hit her face while sunshine glare covered the jungle. She had to hurry up.

"Men at the shore," she muttered. Droops of sweat fell from her forehead when she finally spotted the golf course. Leo and Jordy were in the distance, playing distractedly; they didn't notice her. She tried to yell but didn't have enough air in her lungs.

"Let's do this, son," said Leo with determination, holding his club.

"Yes, Papa."

"Listen you have to find your swing, don't cling to your stick, let it flow, allow it to be an extension of your arms. Do you understand?"

"Jordy wants offer a ball to the lake in sacrifice."

"NO! Come on boy, concentrate. Close your eyes. Listen to the wind, the birds…the branches in the trees."

"Ah, I want to be the best golfer in the world."

"Then, play along with the rhythm of nature, be part of it… Let's make music, boy …Now, open your eyes. What do you hear?" Leo asked him merrily.

"I hear mom calling."

"What?"

"LEONARD!" Finally, Grace shouted breathlessly. He ran to meet her "What's going on? Why do you have my gun?"

She hardly could speak, "Men…. at the shore!"

"How many?"

"Few…Hurry," running fast towards the shore, they almost went out of the jungle.

When suddenly, they stop at the sound of loaded pistols. They turned, and before them, two pirates were pointing guns. They were next to the shelter. With quick determination, Grace threw the rifle into Leo's hands.

Behind huge plants, a man came out. He was carrying Vicky, who was embracing him with familiarity. In his other hand, he had little Julian standing up next to him. The children had candy in their hands, and smiles on their faces, unaware of the danger.

"Governor! We met again," said Red cracking a smile.

"Leave my children alone."

"You're children, ha! What a surprise," he said and saw the infants with hollowed eyes.

"GET OUT OF MY ISLAND."

"No…Governor…You see, we're here for profit. We want gold."

"There's no gold here."

"Ha, ha, ha, did you hear that? The governor says there is no gold in the Treasury Island." Red said to pirates who shared a laugh. Next walked towards Leo threatened, "How much do you think I can get for these cutes in the slavery market?"

"Release them!" Grace yelled and approached him, but Leo seized her arm.

"What we have here?" The pirate saw the woman with lust. "Who's the lady? I want to pay her my respects," he said and took her hand to kiss.

Leonard didn't think twice and shot Red, whose face twitched convulsively and hit the grown dead.

"Run!" Leo pushed Grace away.

Children and mother disappeared in the jungle and in an instant, the other two men shot at her husband in his chest and stomach. Leo's body jumped by the impact and crashed on some bushes. He managed not to lose balance as he felt a fire burning on his body.

A cloud of gun smoke covered him. After seconds the pirates looked for Leo's body on the ground, but instead, they heard a howl coming out of the jungle.

"AAHHH!" Leo was on his feet, feeling range like never before and rushing furiously towards the men who saw him incredulous. He hit them with a stick until they fell to the ground, then lifted off one buccaneer from his ripped shirt and yelled - "LEAVE!"

Both men ran terrorized as they saw Leo bleeding, going after them like a walking death. When he looked for his wife and tried to walk towards her, his legs didn't obey him. The jungle was moving in circles around him, and breathing was impossible. Deep in pain, he touched his stomach; his hands were covered in blood.

"Grace!"

"OH…God." She cried. Their eyes met.

"Take the bullets out, sew the wounds….don't be …." -he didn't finish the sentence and collapsed, fell to the ground unconscious. Grace ran to him and tried to move him. With horror, she saw her husband lying in a pool of blood- "JORDY COME AND HELP ME!" She cried, and they move him inside the hunt.

> *"To die, to sleep. To sleep, perchance to dream- ay,*
> *there's the rub. For in this sleep of death*
> *what dreams may come…"*
> *- Hamlet.*

In the darkest of the night, the crickets were singing loudly.

Leo's eyes were closed. He couldn't move. His breathing was irregular. He probably was unconscious, he wasn't sure, but we could hear and see around him. From above, like he was floating out of his body. Probably he was dreaming.

The children were sleeping. Jordy was sitting next to the fire looking at him with his big eyes full of tears.

Grace was cleaning his wounds. With a knife, she took the remaining bullets from his chest; then she sewed his flesh with thread. Her eyes were wet, and her pulse tremble after cleaning the wounds and removing the dry blood. She placed medicinal leaves on his chest and stomach. Granddaughter of a wise doctor, she had some knowledge of medicine. Nevertheless, she was worried by the amount of blood he was losing. Grace's rosary was on her lap. She prayed all night.

"Come on darling, wake up, love," -Leo could hear her.

She kept him cool with wet rags. The night wind stirred, and the palms were warning of dawn. Leonard was aware of it, but no sound came from his mouth. His eyes remained closed. He was at death's door, in limbo. A cold sensation seized him and projected his body into the universe. He was no longer subject to gravity.

At the speed of a rocket, he found himself in a light tunnel. Shadows with no faces were coming towards him, another flicker and he was walking on a beach. A quiet beach with no sounds and a special light, brighter than the sun. A perfect peace invaded him. It was a glorious day.

An incredible joy filled his heart, but his body wasn't made of matter anymore. He felt light as a feather and connected with everything alive. A young man approached him, probably an angel. Impeccably dressed in shining long clothes. The man was welcoming him with a warm expression. His face was familiar. A sensation of great love invaded him.

"Father…. is it you?"

King Phillipe looked younger. Behind him was his mother smiling with open arms. "MOM!" Leo shouted.

"It is not your time yet, Leonard." The distinctive voice of his father was speaking serene. He wanted to run towards them, but his father stopped him and said, "You can't stay…they need you," Phillipe never opened his mouth yet he spoke thru his mind. At that moment blood came out from Leo's mouth. He opened his eyes, he was coughing. Still, couldn't move.

"Leonard!" Grace cried, cleaning his face, it was almost noon of next day, and the sun was shining. He couldn't speak and felt weak. He stared at Grace. Intense pain was over his chest. He tried to talk.

"I saw them!" He mumbled "They're in Heaven."

"Shhhh. Baby….don't talk…."

"Please, believe me I saw them….there is a Heaven, Grace. I know now!" A splash of blood came from his mouth again.

"Please, baby don't talk. Sweetheart, everything is fine, now." Grace kissed his forehead and felt relieved.

Fifty One

Youth Island

After the incident with the pirates, the island became famous with a legend of an immortal sailor: a mad man who captured exotic parrots, and owned fantastic treasures.

Leo recovered, enjoyed the curiosity and morbid stories about him. With an open chest showing his tattooed scars and hostile attitude; he visited Habanera and talked to a few people only with the purpose of trade.

On day after a visit to Habanera, he indulged his family with a surprise.

"Come and see….the treasure I've found!" said the father proudly.

"What's in this box?" Asked Vicky jumping on a chair.

"You'll know if you solve a riddle."

"Tell us the riddle, papa…tell us," pleaded Julian excitedly. His firstborn was an intuitive and creative fellow. He spent most of the time helping his mother with house projects. His favorite pastime was weaving baskets. The beauty that surrounded him offered a perfect spot to develop his gentle personality.

"Mother, papa is saying a riddle. Come on, hurry!" The little girl shouted excitedly, holding a doll. Vicky grew up free as a bird and curious as a kitten. She had a tremendous facility to learn from books and nature. Intrepid and bold, every day consisted of a great adventure for the bright girl, who showed the stubbornness of her father and the dedication of her mother.

Grace entered the shelter; her spirit was calm after seeing her husband completely recovered, "what's going on?" She asked.

"Inside this box, there is a treasure and the answer to a riddle," said her husband.

"Oh, tell us!" said Grace, placing some flowers on the table.

"If you look at the number in my face, you won't find 13 anyplace….what I am?"

"It's a book!" said Julian.

"No…silly is a doll," guessed Vicky.

"Nor a book neither a doll…it's a clock," answered the young mother.

"Exactly!"

The kids opened the box and were delighted with the piece of art. A hand carved mechanical Black Forest Cuckoo from Germany.

"How did you get this?" Asked Grace amazed.

"You know Habanera. It's full of pirate's treasures."

"I'll be a pirate one day, and I'll bring all types of treasures to my island," shouted Vicky, while holding the Cuckoo in her arms.

Except for Jordy, their appearance didn't change for decades. People were surprised and scared of the legend of the mysterious family that didn't grow old. For that reason, the name of the island changed several times as; *"Isle of Parrots…The Treasure Island and finally The Isle of the Youth."* As a rumor grew that somewhere in the middle of the jungle, was the fountain of eternal youth.

"Don't cry because it is over,
smile because it happened."
- Dr. Seuss

Monarchy

The young father promised his family to move back to the colonies at the end of the Revolutionary war, but months became years, decades, and finally, they got news from, Europe.

"Oh…My Lord!" Grace exclaimed, reading an old publication.

"What's wrong?" Asked Leo.

She shoved the journal on his face, "You knew, didn't you?"

He read the paper and said coldly, "Oh, I did."

"Why you didn't tell me?"

"I forgot," he said careless, and lit his pipe.

"OUR FRIENDS DIED DECAPITATED, AND YOU FORGOT TO MENTION IT!"

"I didn't want to upset you," he said while puffing smoke.

"There's no mistake in this article," she turned the pages, "this is accurate, right?" she asked, dreading the answer.

"Pretty much, the revolutionaries executed both."

"When?"

"The King in January and the Queen this past October."

"Oh!" Her voice faded while remembering, "She was so young when she married."

"She was in her teens…." He remembered sadly.

Grace took a sip of tea, she looked anxious, "What happened to their children?"

"Prison. They might get executed too."

"Praise the Lord!" She said, holding Julian, "On what charges?"

"On the charges of being heirs to the throne." He said, staring at her face.

"What are we going to do, Leonard?"

"Monarchies are in danger now. Just as Cargill predicted. There are conflicts in the entire Continent."

"So, this means….."

"Yes, Grace. I'm sorry. We can't leave the island." He walked away from her.

"You promised me to go back. You probably think I'm putting on vain airs," she stood up and followed him, "But we're royalty!"

"Not, anymore. It's better for us to stay here, disappeared from the map. Left for dead."

A chill ran through her body, "Left for dead?" She whispered with watery eyes while Jordy stood next to her to hug her.

"Safety is first, Grace. We can't risk the children." He turned to her daughter and exclaimed, "Hey, little mermaid, did you get bucket?"

"Don't cry, mommy," pleaded Julian.

Grace cleaned her face and composed. She didn't want to worry her children, "Papa is going to the beach. Hurry, you better get your buckets." She said, hiding her sadness.

The children love to fish, gather shells and seafood in little buckets to run back home and show their accomplishment.

"Listen to your mother. We're bringing her a fest."

"Tomorrow is Christmas!" Noticed Victoria.

"That's right, little girl," Leo exclaimed carrying his daughter on his shoulders. "Are my pirates ready?" He asked the boys, ticking their bellies.

"Aye, Captain." Answer Julian laughing.

"Off, we go...." Leo kissed his wife, blinked, and said "Baby, trust me on this," then closed the door behind them and disappeared tuning a song.

"Fifteen men on a dead man's chest...

Yo ho ho and a bottle of rum...

Drink and the devil be done for the rest...

Yo ho ho and bottle of rum,"

Their happy voices in the distance gave her comfort. Leonard was right; safety was first. At night, after drinking a few glasses of rum, the couple made plans to build an oyster farm to grow pearls, and a small hut to teach crafts to the children. Gentle as the summer breeze, Victoria and Julian grew up surrounded by beauty. For them, sugary beaches and deep crystalline waters were home. Connected to nature, they were hidden in a refuge far from the chaos and violence of civilization.

Fifty two

"The sky shuddered, a mournful silence covered all.
The sun disappeared behind a dark horizon,
and the weeping of a storm became a deadly howl."

On a cloudy afternoon, Grace noticed the animals in the shelter nervous and ready to run away. Not far away, Leo on the beach was concerned when he saw an increase of about six feet in the ocean swell, and the waves growing to an unusual height.

The wind was blowing stronger than ever. *"A storm is approaching!"* -Leo thought and ran to the shelter. He had a hunch. A black cloud of emergency was covering his kingdom. Grace at the shelter was alarmed as the wind could be heard outside blowing strongly. She felt a contraction in her belly; her seven month baby moved violently in her womb. Soon, both parents were shuffling around their belongings, shoving water containers and food into small baskets. Leo saw with concern that the structure of the shelter was not strong enough to guard them against the storm.

"Come on. We're going to the caves," shouted Leo.

"But why?" asked Julian confused. In a matter of minutes, their hut was flooded. Leo was urging his family to abandon their shelter which was creaking announcing a collapse beneath them. They knew at that time, they were hit not by a storm but a fierce hurricane.

"Come on…….everybody move OUT, OUT!" Leo pushed them. Water from the sky came down copiously. The furious wind made it difficult to walk in the heavy rain.

"EVERYBODY RUN," shouted Leo.

Rivers of water formed in the roads carrying strong currents.

"I CAN'T!" Cried Grace, holding Julian, who was covering his eyes from the heavy rain. In a matter of minutes, the water was up to their knees. Leo went back to rush them.

"Come on, hurry to the mountains…" They walked together. Palm trees were torn from the roots, and coconuts were fired like cannonballs.

"The caves, we're here!" Leo finally shouted and turned to them. When he heard Grace scream, "Victoria!... Where's Victoria?" – Her voice was cracking.

"When did we lose her?" Leo asked his wife. The rain became a torrential downfall, and Julian screamed at his parents that Jordy was also missing. Leo left his frantic wife mid-sentence and sprinted downhill, calling his adopted son. The ground avalanched under him as he fell into the thick river of mud that dragged him under the mighty waters. He was barely able to reach a large branch from a nearby tree, still undamaged by the storm. He tried to compose himself and looked around. His heart stopped when he saw the silhouette of Jordy crouching over the flood. Leo ran towards it and realized that his son was desperately trying to grab Victoria, who struggled with all her will to stay over the vicious waters. Just when Jordy was about to catch her, a large log washed down and tumbled her below the surface. Jordy jumped into the river without hesitation. Time stopped as Leo stared at the surface, horrified. Victoria's body was launched forcefully by Jordy, who had barely enough strength to get her out of the rushing water. Her father ran over to pull her to the ground.

"Jordy, Jordy!" Leo shouted while embracing his daughter and waiting an agonizingly long time for any part of Jordy's body to emerge, but he never did, and Leo ran to the caves with her daughter on his arms.

"Where's Jordy?" Asked Grace, concerned.

Leo nodded his head and didn't answer. The wind howled like a wolf pack. The palm trees were still bending, and the heavy rain didn't cede. Soon, darkness covered it all. They sat inside a cave around a campfire. The storm lasted all night and part of the next morning. By midday, the sky was clear, and the sun was shining again, but the island was not the same. When they returned to the hut, they stopped frozen at the entrance of what used to be their home.

The place looked like a giant had stepped on it, destroying all in his path. The grief they felt was devastating. Everything was broken and in bad condition. A small stream of water ran through the shelter.

Grace and the kids moved the debris and tried to save some of their treasures.

"What are you hiding? What did you find?" Asked Vicky to her brother, who was pail with his arms behind his back. "Nothing," answered Julian trying to hide her destroyed diary and her favorite doll.

"Look…the cuckoo is broken," observed Vicky devastated. "It is completely destroyed." She held it with one hand.

"Everything is lost," affirmed Julian holding back tears.

"Oh, my God!" Muttered Grace when she saw her husband.

Leo appeared on the horizon carrying the lifeless body of his adopted son. They ran towards him and immediately felt intense grief. There were no possessions as valuable as Jordy's life. Everybody gathered around the lifeless body of beloved Jordy.

"Is he dead, papa?" Asked Julian.

"Yes, son." Answered Leo and placed the body gently on the ground, "We must bury him." Said Grace with watery eyes.

Leo dug a grave and took the time to finish engraving a polished stone, placed as a tribute. Grace asked to bury him in the same spot they met him. The children placed on his tomb his favorite golf clubs and toys.

The stone read: "HERE REST OUR BELOVED SON, JORDY…THE WORLD BEST GOLFER."

"I'm going to miss him so much," said Grace wiping tears.

"We all are, darling." Said her husband knowing, that he was not only burying his son but a perfect stage of their lives. A stage that would never repeat again. His only desire, at that moment, was to be able to share time again with Jordy, somehow, somewhere.

"You saved me, dear brother," Vicky remembered sadly, leaving some tropical flowers on his tomb. "Thank you…."

They sat at Jordy's tomb and remained quiet for some minutes.

Their hearts were broken, but Leo was impaired, immobile without straight in his legs as he mentally toured his island: his golf course, the shelter, the crafts school, the oysters' farm, everything was damaged. The loss was complete, and restoration was impossible. He stood up and offered a hand to his wife to get on her feet.

"It's time!" Exhaled Leo finally, feeling an urge to leave the island-"We pack anything in a good state, and we'll leave as soon as possible." Grace smiled at him, relieved. It was time to re-direct their destination.

"We'll embark in Habanera towards to the colonies." He informed them.

"The United States, papa!" Julian corrected him with a heart full of excitement.

Leonardo King Baylor

While disembarking from a small ship at the New York port of entry, the family had a combination of excitement and curiosity for the new world. Carrying baskets and bundles of cloth, they walked among a multitude of people who pushed them rapidly to the entrance of a free country. Leo was distracted by the idea of a government from the people based on justice and liberty. They continued strolling into a multitude in reverent silence. It was cold, and winter was sprinkling snowflakes. Soon, Leo was in front of a man in uniform. An Immigration Officer was looking at him with small spectacles behind a window.

"Name?" The man asked him severely. "Country of origin? Show me your documents!" He inquired.

"Oh, yes. Leonard..oh…documents?

"Leonardo, what?"

"Leonardo what?" He repeated amused.

"That's what I said, Sir. What is your last name?"

"King!" Cried Grace in the back.

"Did you say King?"

"Yes, of course…King."

"From where?.....Sir?"

"BayCastle." Grace interfered, again. "We're from Nordland from The House of BayCastle."

"I beg your pardon?"

"Excuse me officer," Leo's face glowed and firmly said, "The name is Bay…lor. I'm Leonardo King Baylor, immigrant…. and this is my family."